MURDER EXPRESS

Other books by Robert Scott:

Lost Youth
Advertising Murder

MURDER EXPRESS

•

Robert Scott

AVALON BOOKS
NEW YORK

110708

F
Sco

Library of Congress Cataloging-in-Publication Data
Scott, Robert, 1947–
    Murder express / Robert Scott.
        p.   cm.
    ISBN 978-0-8034-9928-7 (acid-free paper)   1. Private
investigators—British Columbia—Vancouver—Fiction.
2. Ex-police officers—Fiction.   3. Vancouver (B. C.)—Fiction.
4. Murder—Investigation—Fiction.   5. Railroad travel—
Fiction.   I. Title.
    PS3619.C6835M87   2008
    813'.6—dc22   2008023180

PRINTED IN THE UNITED STATES OF AMERICA
ON ACID-FREE PAPER
BY HADDON CRAFTSMEN, BLOOMSBURG, PENNSYLVANIA

To the real "soon to be Doctor Nadia." You are an inspiration. We've laughed and cried together. We've been family and shared family. I know you will succeed in all you do. I am so proud of you.

Todo va a estar bien!

THANKS:

To my writing buddies at the Words R Us writing group in Colwood: Thanks for all your suggestions as, together, we have encouraged one another. Thanks for your friendship through the years. Thanks for sharing your stories. I'll miss you all, and our Tuesday mornings together.

I would also like to acknowledge Dr. D. P. Lyle, M.D., author of *Murder and Mayhem: A Doctor Answers Medical and Forensic Questions for Mystery Writers.* Not only are his books authoritative and informative, but when there has been a question needing an expert's answer, Dr. Lyle has welcomed e-mail queries and given a personal response within twenty-four hours.

As always, this book would not be possible without the labours of the good folks at Avalon Books. For more than half a century, they have worked tirelessly to bring, to readers like you, wholesome entertainment. Together with them, I hope we continue to succeed in that task.

And finally, to you, dear reader, my heartfelt thanks for picking up this humble tome. It wouldn't be nearly so much fun to write without you.

Prologue

The gentle rocking of the railway coach had a soothing effect on the passengers as the tourist train rumbled along. Outside the window, the view of the mountains was breathtaking. This was the second, and last, day of the journey that had begun only twenty-four hours earlier.

Not all of the passengers were fully awake. Some swayed in their seats as they looked out at the passing scenery. Others stood in the aisles, speaking to coach mates and new acquaintances.

Oscar Dempster also swayed back and forth with the rocking of the train. His eyes bulged from their sockets. His tongue protruded from his mouth. Oscar was going to miss a fine breakfast. In fact, he was going to miss the rest of the trip. To tell the truth he was going to miss the rest of what might have been left of his life.

A length of nylon rope was looped around the fleshy neck of the man from California. He was sitting, awkwardly splayed, on the floor of the spacious washroom that had been provided for the comfort of passengers on the *Last Spike Special.*

Few people were going to be comfortable on this day's journey into Calgary.

"My husband has been gone a long time," the lady with the grey hair and bright-red lipstick said to the young woman kneeling on the seat and leaning over the backrest.

"Maybe he's reading in there," the younger woman said. "My husband always takes a magazine with him. He's new. I'll have to try to break him of the habit."

She was tall and looked fit. Her long blond hair hung over her shoulders. Her husband sat, looking out the window, apparently unconcerned that the older lady's husband was too long in the lavatory or that his own new wife had plans to reform him.

"Well, if he's not back soon," the older woman said, "I'll have to go after him. He's missing the view."

Farther down the coach, a frail-looking little man turned toward the washroom door and stepped through the opening.

The bloodcurdling scream that followed seemed uncharacteristic for one who appeared so feeble of frame. The speed with which he exited the washroom was even more surprising.

"There's a dead guy in there!" Bob Benson yelled as he pulled himself up the aisle, using the seat backs for support.

He did an enviable job of fighting the forward momentum of the train as he headed toward the front of the coach. The attendant, Stewart, had rushed from his supply room, where he had been preparing breakfast trays, when Mr. Benson's cry of terror had gone up.

"Oh nuts," the new husband said to his wife, not thinking about the conversation she had been having with the lady behind her. "Just when I thought we were going to have a restful honeymoon, some guy decides to go bananas in the bathroom."

"Dear, I think maybe we should wait and see what made that poor man so upset. He looked kind of scared," the young woman said, as she patted her husband on the shoulder and gave him a sympathetic look. It was then that she realized Mrs. Dempster was heading for the door that Bob Benson had just come out of in such a rush.

"Uh, Ruby—Mrs. Dempster—I think it might be best if you waited for a moment."

It was too late. Ruby Dempster screamed almost as loud as the little man who had preceded her.

By the time the younger woman arrived at the door, Ruby's red lips were parted in terror, as she stared at the body rocking back and forth with the rhythm of the rails.

Chapter One

T TWENTY-FOUR HOURS EARLIER . . .
he happy couple sitting at the window of the coach was obviously in love. The way that they looked at each other told the story. The way they held hands confirmed the fact.

Jack Elton and Valerie Cummins were more than in love, they were married. Of course, the one had led to the other, but it had come as a surprise to both of them when Jack proposed and Valerie accepted.

This was their honeymoon trip. Jack had always liked trains, and Valerie had liked Jack since the moment they met. They had agreed that it was meant to be.

"I'm glad we were able to get tickets," Jack said. "I'm looking forward to the trip. It sure is nice to be away from the office and the work, and to be able to relax with my wife."

It still seemed strange to him, to be referring to Val as his wife.

There had been times when, as a private investigator, Jack had questioned the wisdom of marriage. The work was uncertain. The hours could be long. There would be times when he was away from home for extended periods.

A recent trip, before he proposed, had almost led to the end of a beautiful friendship. Jack had been on assignment for a man who wanted to retrieve his daughter from a kidnapper. Val had not been happy that he would have to go away. And Jack had soon discovered that he didn't want to stay away too long. It had solidified his resolve and resulted in his proposal to the woman who now rode with him on a train trip through a most beautiful part of North America.

"I can't say I'm missing my patrol car either," Valerie replied.

Jack's most recent occupation was as a member of the Vancouver Police Victim Services Unit.

Before that, he had tried his hand at being a private eye. It had been satisfying work, but without the full force of the law behind him, Jack had discovered that his investigations were slowed by the need to be constantly referring back to his former buddies in the detective division.

"Former" because there had been a little unpleasantness about his ability to "serve and protect" a few years earlier. He had been relieved of duty under a cloud of suspicion over a bad drug bust. It was rumored that he had been using his job as a cover to traffic in drugs. And while some of his coworkers had supported him, there were others who wanted to believe the worst. It had been a tough fight, but now he was back at the work he loved, with the record finally wiped clean. He could thank his former boss, Ted Brown, for that. Ted had gone to bat for him when Jack had finally decided to swallow his pride and asked for a review of his file.

It was true that what he was doing now involved a lot of desk work. He wasn't as immersed in the action as he would have liked to be. But he did have a job that allowed him to investigate crimes. He got to speak to the victims and to help them deal with their traumas. Sometimes he helped with the task of determining who was guilty of the crimes.

He was satisfied with his lot in life.

For now, he and Valerie could leave work behind, and were looking forward to this trip that would take them through the Rocky Mountains, stopping at places of interest along the way.

This was no ordinary railroad on which the newlyweds were traveling. They had been careful to avoid the transcontinental, government-owned railway and had chosen instead a company that was in the business of providing a real vacation. The *Last Spike Special* was an anniversary train of sorts. It had first been created in 1985 to commemorate the driving of the last spike of the new railroad that had been built from sea to sea in Canada one hundred years earlier. The tourist train had been so successful that it was revived ten years later, and had been running every July since then.

Everyone on the *Last Spike Special* was here for the enjoyment of the trip. They would be eating together in the dining coach. Their attendant would point out places of interest and talk about the history of the towns and villages they passed through.

At night the train would stop, and they would spend the evening in a hotel. The next morning, the passengers would be together again, having breakfast as their train moved on to its final destination.

It was going to be a wonderful, relaxing trip. Or so Jack thought.

Through the window, Jack and Val could see more travelers moving along the platform. Some of these folks would be their coach mates. Jack and Val had discussed the trip since the day it had been planned. One thing they agreed on was that they wanted to be vacationing with agreeable people.

Jack had taken the trip once before, by himself. He had regretted that decision almost from the moment the train left the station.

A group of eight, traveling together, had ruined the ride by playing cards and talking while the attendant was attempting to give the other vacationers some interesting commentary. Jack had wondered how people, paying as much money as these were, could waste their time by avoiding the spectacular scenery and ignoring the fascinating details about what they would have seen, if only they had cared.

Jack had begun to believe that he and Val would be spared a similar fate, but his faith was not rewarded for very long.

The coach was almost full. In fact there were only two seats left, right behind the Eltons. With only moments left before the train was to leave the station, Val pointed out the window.

"Look at that couple, Jack," she said. "They don't look to be having too good a time."

Out on the platform, a rather large man appeared to be berating his wife as the two struggled to drag overloaded suitcases to the one remaining open door—the one leading up the steps into the coach where the only available space was behind Jack and Valerie.

Their voices and attitudes preceded them down the aisle.

"Sir? Ma'am? I'm terribly sorry, but you can't take those suitcases to your seat. They are supposed to be checked onto the baggage car when you arrive at the station to board."

It was evident that the attendant was exercising great restraint with these passengers who had ignored the instruction, which surely had been given to them in both verbal and written form when they had booked their trip.

The new guests were not nearly as well controlled.

"What kind of a ship are you guys runnin' here, sonny? I'm on vacation, and I couldn't get a drink in the station. Don't you folks have any booze in this town?"

It seemed to escape the man's notice that it was barely nine in the morning.

"This trip is going to be interesting," Jack whispered to Val, who just crossed her arms and shook her head.

The attendant managed to convince the man of the wisdom of having the bags taken to the baggage coach at the front of the train. He invited them to have a seat.

"You might as well sit by the window," the man said to the woman who was obviously his wife. "I don't know why I let you talk me into taking this trip. I sure hope there are some good casinos with well-stocked bars, along this route. At least then it won't be a total loss. Hey, sonny, you got anything to drink?"

"Certainly, sir," came the reply. "Would you like some orange juice?"

The thick silence that followed the exchange convinced Jack that the answer was a definite no.

The train started to move. In spite of the recent disturbance, Jack still held out hope that the trip could be an enjoyable one.

The man in the seat behind Jack and Valerie sat looking straight ahead as the coach left the station.

The attendant stood at the end of the aisle and clicked on a portable microphone.

"Good morning, ladies and gentlemen," he began.

"Welcome aboard the *Last Spike Special*. My name is Stewart and I'll be your tour guide during this trip. Sit back and relax. If you need anything, just let me know.

"If you look out the right side of the coach now, you'll see the first sight of interest."

Everyone looked to see. Everyone, that is, except for the man in the seat behind the newlyweds.

Stewart continued. "That, ladies and gentlemen, is our station crew. They have to stay at home and help folks just like you make reservations for the other trips that will be taking place this month."

Outside the coach, a small group of young men and women, dressed in maroon blazers and grey slacks or skirts, waved excitedly at the passing windows.

"Juvenile," the angry man said, and folded his arms over his ample chest.

As the train rolled along, through the countryside and into the Fraser Valley, east of Vancouver, Stewart busied himself with preparations for the continental breakfast that would be served in what was called Adventurer Class.

Passengers in these coaches did not have some of the amenities that those in Discovery Class received. Nor, Jack considered, did they have quite as impressive a credit card bill awaiting them when they returned from their luxury rail trip.

Actually, he thought, *apart from dining car service and the opportunity to ride in a scenic dome, there was little to separate the Adventurers from the Discoverers.*

Now that he was responsible for the travel expenses of his wife, Jack was more convinced than ever that the lower-priced trip was the better deal.

The man in the seat behind him was complaining again.

"Why do they have to travel so slowly? Can't they pick up the pace a little? I thought the whole idea was to get from one place to another."

"Oh, Oscar. Relax. We'll be there soon enough," his wife was saying. "We can go hunting for a nice casino, and then you'll be happy."

She proceeded to fish around in a large purse and drew out a compact and a tube of bright-red lipstick. She busied herself with the application of the makeup.

"They are quite a pair," Jack whispered to Val, who was gazing at the passing scenery.

"What's that?" she asked, obviously distracted. "What are you talking about?"

"Never mind," Jack said, and watched as Stewart made his way down the aisle with his cart, which was loaded with juices, pastries, cereals, tea, and coffee.

What looked appealing to Jack did not strike the fancy of the man named Oscar.

"Jeez, is that all you've got?"

Stewart tried his best to be courteous to his demanding passenger. It was obvious that this promised to be a challenging trip.

"Would you like some juice? Coffee? Tea? Anything from the cart?"

Stewart is truly handling the situation quite well, Jack thought.

"Well, I guess I'd better have something," the man said. "I've gotta take my pills. Bum ticker. This trip's gonna be the death of me. Gimme some orange juice."

Jack was beginning to have murderous thoughts, and he hadn't even met the man. He wondered what was going through the mind of the young man with the food cart, who was being paid to smile and be courteous to the likes of Oscar what's-his-name.

When Stewart approached the Eltons, Jack smiled up at him, nodded toward the seat behind, and gave a knowing wink. Stewart gave a noncommittal shrug and asked if he or Valerie would like something for breakfast.

They made their selections. Jack and Valerie spoke little as they ate. The sights that were passing by the window gave them a new appreciation for the place where they lived. This was their province.

After they finished the morning meal and Stewart collected plates, cutlery, and the wads of wrapping from muffins and pastries, those who were destined to share the trip in the same coach began to move about, introducing themselves and expressing their appreciation for both the beauty of the countryside and the luxury of train travel.

Stewart appeared well-versed in the history of the villages and towns through which the *Last Spike Special* was passing. He also told his *guests*—that was the term he used—about the wildlife along the track, and urged them to call out if they saw something of interest.

It was not long before Jack and Valerie learned that the coach mates behind them were Oscar and Ruby Dempster. They were from Simi Valley, California, and Oscar was unimpressed so far.

Oscar had spent most of his adult life selling cars and was now retired.

"I'd just about had it with bad-tempered clients," he said. "Hard to please 'em. And they always wanted something for nothing. So, after fifty years in the business, I finally sold out, a couple months ago. Of course, the fact that I got this bad heart made the decision a little easier. Doctor wanted me to give up drinking, smoking, and fatty foods. Well, I don't smoke anymore. The little woman, here, made sure of that. Couldn't get a moment's peace till I quit."

Jack didn't have the courage to ask how the two of them were enjoying their trip.

"How are you enjoying the trip?" Valerie asked.

"Not bad," Oscar replied. "Between you and me, though, I think we got taken. This is a pretty slow train. I want to get where the action is."

"Not me," Val said. "I came on this trip to enjoy the scenery and the rail travel itself. I live a pretty hectic life most of the time. I like this. I'm being served. I don't have cooking or dishes to do. And I've got good company to travel with."

She looked up at Jack and gave him a wink and a smile.

"Well, I guess you've got your wish," Oscar said, and sat down heavily beside his wife, who just patted the man's knee and smiled at the young couple.

An older man came down the aisle, nodding to various passengers and shaking hands with some as he introduced himself.

Jack was still standing beside the seats occupied by the Dempsters when the gentleman arrived.

"Hi there," Jack said, and held out his hand.

"Hello to you," the man said. "I'm William, William Marshall. Judge William Marshall. Don't call me Bill or Willie. I like William. More dignified, I think. For a judge, I mean."

With that he reared back and laughed.

Sounds completely undignified, Jack thought, *for a judge, I mean.*

"My name's Jack," he said. "And this is my wife, Valerie."

Valerie smiled and turned again to her window gazing.

The Dempsters were making no effort to make themselves known, so Jack decided to take the initiative.

"These are the Dempsters, Oscar and Ruby. Have you met?"

"I don't think so," Oscar Dempster said.

William Marshall just shrugged and moved farther down the aisle, shaking hands as he went and adding, from time to time, "Don't call me Bill or Willie. I like

William. More dignified, I think. For a judge, I mean," followed by the uncharacteristic laugh.

Bob Benson was a businessman from Toronto. He and his wife had flown in a couple of days before, to tour Vancouver and Victoria. They were taking the trip to Calgary to enjoy a few relaxing days before jetting back east, where Bob would go back to his high-pressure desk job for an automotive supply chain.

Pat Benson, Bob's wife, was a stay-at-home mother of two children—boys—aged three and five. The kids were with their grandparents for a week.

"I hope my mom and dad survive the experience," the fit-looking brunet said with a shake of her head. "It's all I can do to keep up with them these days."

Before long, it was time for another meal. The socializing would have to continue later.

Stewart was busy shepherding his little flock back to their seats, urging them to lower their table trays for a lunch that included a substantial serving of cold roast beef on a crusty bun, along with a selection of cheeses and fresh salads.

Oscar Dempster was moderately happy at the opportunity to have something stronger than tea or coffee with his meal. But he remained less than impressed with his experience when he learned that he would be severely limited in the amount he could drink.

This being a family-oriented experience, the intention of which was to allow everyone to enjoy the trip, it was felt essential by the *Last Spike Special Company* to restrict its passengers' consumption of anything that might make them less civilized.

No one wanted Oscar to be more obnoxious than he already appeared to be and they quietly cheered Stewart's handling of the situation.

"You mean to say, all I get is one lousy drink with my meal?" Dempster asked.

"Sorry, sir, that's it for now. I'll be happy to serve you again next time."

Before Oscar could say another word, the coach attendant wheeled his cart to the front and began stowing boxes and cans in the little office that was his only refuge in times of need.

It would prove more useful to the young man as the afternoon progressed.

Chapter Two

"*Beyond Hope, but not quite at Hell's Gate.*" That was where the passengers on the *Last Spike Special* found themselves, as they settled in for their first afternoon.

The fur traders who traveled the trails more than one hundred and fifty years before had named the town, at the junction of the Fraser and the Coquihalla Rivers, Fort Hope. They had expected that it would mark an easier route for their journeys. Ten years later, the gold rush brought more people but reduced fur trading to almost nothing.

Jack knew this because he had read the blurb in a leaflet that had been left on every seat for the passengers who had boarded that morning.

The town had also served as the location for Sylvester

Stallone's first *Rambo* movie and, by mid-morning, it was behind them.

Now, as the trip progressed, they were coming to the gorge called Hell's Gate, where an estimated two hundred million gallons of water rage through a narrowing of the Fraser River every minute.

Jack watched in fascination as the gondola cars of the AirTram carried sightseers from one side to the other, five hundred feet above the water.

A shudder went through him as his gaze shifted from the wires suspending the tram to the water pounding against the rocks below.

"Can you imaging what it would be like to get caught in that?" he asked his wife, tilting his head in the direction of the gorge.

"Not really," Val replied, without looking away from the window that had claimed her attention for most of the trip to that point.

"You wouldn't know what hit you," Jack said.

"Well, you probably would. But I don't think you'd know much after that."

Val smiled. Jack watched her face reflected in the pane of glass.

The coach had grown quiet now that the noon meal was over and Stewart had cleaned up most of the trays. The majority of the passengers had risen quite early in order to make their appointment with the sleek maroon-and-silver train that was now drawing them through this great adventure. They sat back, looking satisfied and relaxed.

Jack was thinking that it was nice not to have to drive.

Oscar Dempster was raging like the waters of Hell's Gate about how slow the train was moving, apparently oblivious to those who had paid to be sure that they would not just be watching the now useless telegraph poles whistle past their windows. Modern technology had removed the need for messages to be sent along suspended wires. This was evident from the portable radios that the trainman and conductor carried to communicate with each other and with the engineer in the cab of the diesel that led the procession of rail cars.

Jack begged Valerie to excuse him so he could stand in the vestibule of the coach to take pictures and feel the wind in his face. She dismissed him with a nod and a wave of her hand, still too absorbed in her own sightseeing to feel she was being abandoned.

Jack was thankful to get out of his seat and to be somewhere that Oscar Dempster wasn't. It took a certain spirit of adventure to embark on one of these trips. It seemed that the Dempsters didn't have it.

Maybe, Jack thought, trying to give Oscar the benefit of the doubt, *they were led to believe that this was the same train that makes the transcontinental run twice a week.*

It would make sense to complain about the slowness of the trip if you thought you were traveling on that train. Folks expected to be delivered to their destination in reasonable time.

Of course, if you want to be some place in a real

hurry, rail travel should not be your first choice, he reminded himself, as he pushed through the door of the
coach and was immediately engulfed by the sound of
steel against steel, accompanied by the rush of air created by the train's forward progress.

He pressed his back against the cool metal of the
coach and leaned out the top half of the door as far as
he dared. From this vantage point, Jack was able to get
a sense of what it must be like to ride up front, with the
diesel generators throbbing in the engine compartment
behind the small cab of the engine.

While he was not able to see straight ahead, he was
able to watch as signal standards came into view and
switched from green to yellow and then to red, as the
head end passed over the switches.

He watched as mileposts swept by, announcing to
anyone who cared that regardless of what anyone
thought, the *Last Spike Special* was making progress
toward its stop for the evening.

From time to time they would pass a switchyard or encounter a freight train where the rail was double tracked.
Jack was careful to keep an eye out for those occasions
and to have his camera ready.

One of his wedding gifts had been a new digital re-
flex apparatus. He was giving it a good workout and
was glad that there was no need to change film.

*I only hope the batteries hold out until I have a
chance to recharge,* he thought.

Every once in a while, Jack would look through the

window in the door leading back into the coach. He could see his fellow passengers in various relaxed postures. Now and then, they would stand and stretch, or step into the aisle and walk back and forth.

Jack was startled to feel a hand on his shoulder as he stood with his camera at the ready in the vestibule doorway.

The hand was connected to Judge William Marshall. The judge appeared to have come from the coach behind the one both he and Jack occupied.

"Remember me?" the jurist asked, grinning at Jack.

"Judge William, not Bill or Willie, I presume," Jack said with a small bow.

"Hah! Ya got that right," Marshall said, showing a perfect set of teeth that Jack figured, whether original equipment or not, had set the good lawyer back a fair number of per diems.

"Wonderful trip. Wonderful trip," the judge continued, pressing on into the forward coach and finishing with his signature laugh.

Jack watched him go and wondered what stories the man might be able to tell. Perhaps it was worth pursuing at some point during the trip. Judge William Marshall was a man of some renown.

He was well known in legal circles. His fame preceded even his laugh. Marshall was one of the toughest jurists in the country. Had the law not changed all across Canada thirty years previous, it is likely that Judge William "The Hangman" Marshall would still live up to the name that had been applied before the 1976 vote that abolished capital punishment.

Perhaps things would slow down over the next day, Jack thought, although he doubted it. Then he reflected on how there might be an opportunity to pick Judge Marshall's brain that evening at the hotel. Jack had nothing planned once they stopped for the night. He didn't know what Valerie had in mind, though. There was a live theatre in town and they hadn't been able to get out together until now.

Have to wait and see, Jack thought.

"What do you mean, we have to arrange our own meals tonight?"

Jack had returned from an afternoon of pretending to be an engineer to find Oscar Dempster still at his old trick of challenging Stewart and successfully alienating the rest of the passengers.

Valerie explained to Jack that the man had given his opinion of the country where he was now a guest and had branded it "nothing but wilderness." She confessed that she would gladly assist anyone who wanted to toss the man out and help Oscar see the countryside up close.

He had challenged the political leanings of Toulouse Gravelle, a politician from the east who was known to be a pacifist. Oscar had strong opinions about whole nations of people who didn't see things his way and thought Gravelle should stop "pussy footing" around, as he called it. Before that debate was over, it seemed that Oscar had aroused a certain amount of militancy, against himself, in the heart of the politician.

And now, the man from Simi Valley was chewing out Stewart again because the train would be arriving before the dinner hour and passengers would be expected to make their own eating arrangements.

The man who had been in such a rush to get to his destination now wanted to halt the proceedings so he wouldn't have to go too far afield for his next meal.

On top of all that, he had begun to berate his wife. She appeared to be on the verge of tears.

She begged him to stop treating her like this.

He refused.

Judge Marshall just looked on with an expression of disgust on his face. He shook his head and rubbed his hands together.

Jack wondered who might have the upper hand if the two men were to meet in a court of law.

"I want to talk to that judge," he whispered to Valerie. "I've heard a lot about him. He's made quite a name for himself with some of his controversial decisions."

"Want to make a court case out of it?" she replied.

Jack smiled.

Chapter Three

"**I** think we are too soft on criminals. It would be fine with me if we just put them out of our misery. And I didn't misspeak there. I meant to say 'our misery.' I think that some of these folks are more trouble than they are worth when we put them in prison. With all this modern garbage about the rights of prisoners and the quest for political correctness, I think we're making them a worse burden on society than they were when they were free."

Judge William Marshall was exercising his right of free speech as he and Jack sat, drinking decaf coffee, in the small cafe of their motel.

Their train had been met by a fleet of buses at the railroad station in Kamloops, where they had stopped for the evening. Passengers had been whisked away to their accommodations for the evening. Those who could afford it, those in Discovery Class, were billeted in five-star hotels. The folks in the lower-priced Adventurer Class soon discovered that their digs for the evening were quite acceptable and that, since most of the time would be spent sleeping, a comfortable bed was all that was really needed.

Val had decided to retire early. The trip, though pleasant, was tiring, and she had been up earlier than Jack to pack for the trip that morning.

Jack had decided to go for coffee and had found the judge nursing a white ceramic cup while he perused the local newspaper. He was intrigued by the man who had made such a reputation for himself with his stern lectures to the accused and the severe punishments he handed out. William Marshall was a maximum sentence kind of guy. He had been sorry to see the abolition of the death penalty. This night he was demonstrating that he had mellowed not one iota.

"What do you think we should be doing with convicted criminals?" Jack asked, knowing what the answer would be.

"Take them out of circulation for a very long time," the jurist replied. "Thieves should be put in some sort of program where they have to work to pay back society. By that, I mean they should have to earn real money to pay back their victims. A conviction is some consolation, but without a material way to compensate the folks who have had their stuff stolen, there is still inequity, as far as I'm concerned."

"I guess you've had some interesting cases to adjudicate," Jack said. His questioning tone indicated, he hoped, that he would like to hear some of the judge's stories.

"Well, I'll tell you, there have been some tough ones. Of course, back in the early days, I had to deal with traffic infractions. Sort of a beginner's obligation, if you know what I mean. But, of course you would. You probably had to do traffic court yourself as a police officer."

"You're right about that," Jack admitted. "Some of my most boring moments were spent dealing with the speeders and the drunks. After awhile I realized that some of the same faces were appearing on a regular basis."

"Tell me about it," Marshall said with a shake of the head.

He continued, "Then again, I've overseen trials for theft and fraud. I've sentenced murderers and wife beaters and child molesters. And I've wondered if I got it right, a lot of times. I've questioned whether the court system has done enough. But I'm past that now. I retired last month. This trip is my celebration."

"You're traveling alone?" Jack asked.

"My wife died a couple of years ago. She was sick for a long time. I am fortunate to have a daughter and son-in-law who were able to care for her. They live alone and have a large home. Perhaps you'll have an opportunity to meet them some time. My son-in-law's a police officer."

"Hey. I remember you guys. You're both on the same train as me."

The voice came from behind Jack, but even without turning around, he could tell from the accent of the speaker that it was Toulouse Gravelle, the French Canadian politician.

The new arrival walked up to the table and thrust out his hand to Jack.

"I'm Toulouse Gravelle. You can call me Luce. That's what my *amis,* uh, my friends, call me."

"I know who you are, Luce. I've seen you on TV. I'm Jack Elton, and this is Judge William Marshall." He gestured toward his companion.

"William. Not Bill, or Billy, or Willie," the older man said, and laughed as he had when he was glad-handing his coach mates earlier in the day.

"I'll try to remember that," Gravelle said. "May I join you?"

Jack slid over on the bench, whose vinyl upholstery had been polished to a fine sheen by the posteriors of countless customers who had spent time in the small eatery in days gone by. "Be my guest," he said.

"Whaddaya think of that guy who was complaining all day?" the politician asked.

"He sure has an attitude," Marshall replied. "I wish he'd just be quiet."

"I'm on my honeymoon. I'm trying to have an enjoyable trip with my wife, but I find it hard to stay in the coach when he's ranting on like that," Jack added.

"You're lucky," Gravelle said. "I tried to talk to him and introduced myself. We got into a conversation, and he started arguing with me. He said some pretty nasty things. I have to admit, I've had some treacherous thoughts this afternoon. I don't think I'm quite over his attacks."

"Be careful, there," the judge interjected. "Bad thoughts can lead to bad actions. I've seen people kill for less."

Gravelle gave a nervous laugh.

Just then a waitress arrived to take his order.

When she left to get the politician's toast and a fresh pot of coffee, the conversation turned to other things.

Jack was happy to deal with something other than Judge Marshall's displeasure with the legal system or Oscar Dempster's displeasure with just about everything else.

After the coffee had arrived and the empty cups had been recharged, the three men settled into a conversation about the trip so far and about the fascinating history of the area they had passed through since leaving Vancouver.

When Jack looked at his watch, he was surprised to see that it was past ten. His thoughts turned to Val, sleeping alone in their room.

If she wakes up and sees I'm still gone, she'll wonder what's happened, he thought.

"We have another early morning tomorrow," he said. "I've got to get some sleep, or I'll be no use at all. I'll let you men continue your conversation. I'll see you both in the morning."

As he headed back to his room, Jack was hoping he would be able to enjoy an uncharacteristically sound sleep in a strange bed.

Chapter Four

J ack had not got his wish.

Though the bed was comfortable, his mind would not shut off long enough to let him get a decent sleep.

It had always been this way for Jack. No matter how tired, the first night in a strange bed promised to be a frustrating one. He suspected that, on those rare occasions when he spent more than one day in the same place, it was more the fatigue than anything else that enabled him to sleep better the second night.

When the clock radio came to life—too early for his liking—he dragged himself to an upright position, thankful that he and Val had planned to spend a few days in Calgary in the same hotel. After one more night of tossing, he was fairly confident that he would get a decent sleep in the days that followed.

Val had been up for some time, by the look of things. The bags were packed. Jack's wardrobe for the day was laid out on Val's bed, which was made, in spite of the fact that the housekeeping crew would completely strip it when the Eltons left for the remainder of their trip.

Val wasn't there. Jack wondered where she might be but then remembered that there was a continental breakfast being served to guests of the motel.

A few moments later, there was a soft knock at the door. When Jack answered it, he found his wife with a tray that bore two paper cups of steaming coffee along with pastries and toast from the little kitchenette by the registration desk.

"How was your night?" he asked, after taking the tray from Valerie and setting it on the table by the window.

"I disappeared the moment my head hit the pillow," she answered. "How about you?"

"Slept like a baby," Jack said, with a faint smile. "Laid down for an hour and then was wide awake. Drifted off and was awake again in an hour. Fell asleep for awhile and then—"

"I get the picture," Val interrupted. "It's going to seem like a long day. Good thing you don't have to do the driving. You can just sit back and relax and watch the world go by. You're on vacation."

It was not to be.

The bus came and drove their coach-load to the station, where it discharged them onto the platform.

In spite of his fatigue, Jack was feeling satisfied and

happy. After all, he was traveling with his best friend, the woman he loved, who had signed on to share the ups and downs for the rest of their lives together. No matter what might come his way, he knew he would be able to handle it with Val by his side. He didn't know then how soon that theory was going to be challenged.

Back on their coach, they found that the cleaning crews had done a thorough job the night before. The floors had been washed. The windows were streak free. The seats had been tidied. All was ready for the continuation of the trip.

The railway had learned, during their short life in the tourism business, there would always be one straggler who would oversleep or get sidetracked in the souvenir shop of their previous night's lodging.

There would usually be one load of passengers who were late arriving at the station at the beginning of the second day of the trip. For that reason, passengers were given an early arrival time and the shuttle bus drivers were given some leeway on their departure times.

This day appeared to be no different. But it was passengers from another coach that were the cause of the delay. Everyone sharing the coach with the Eltons was present and accounted for. At least, that was the case until the nasty business of Oscar Dempster's demise.

The train had not been out of the station for more than an hour before the lifeless body of the man from

Simi Valley was discovered in the washroom at the back of the coach.

When Bob Benson had struggled down the aisle, announcing to all that there was a dead body in the lavatory, Ruby Dempster had gone to verify his assertion. Unfortunately, she witnessed the terrible truth that, had he been alive, Oscar would have judged this the worst day of his life.

When the cries of alarm had gone up, Stewart was the first to react in a positive way. As he made his way down the coach, he advised everyone to stay in their seats and to remain calm. When some of the travelers appeared to be ready to disobey his instructions, he would gently back them up and into their seats again, moving so that they could not impede his forward progress. He could do nothing to make people calm, of course, but, he was successfully taking control of the situation, as he had been trained to do.

Val had gone after Ruby Dempster and managed to get her away from the open washroom door. The two were returning to their places.

Jack just shook his head in disbelief.

Trouble seems to find me, wherever I go, he thought. Then he stood up and, as Stewart came toward him, stepped into the aisle and faced the attendant.

"Excuse me, sir. You'll have to sit down. I need for everyone to remain in their seats. We'll be stopping at the next station and—"

"I know all that," Jack said. "I was just going to ask

you if you needed any help. I'm a police officer. Perhaps I can be of some assistance."

Stewart looked doubtful.

"Well, alright. Maybe you could start by keeping people in their seats. I have to get to the end of the coach and deal with this."

Jack nodded and moved aside to let Stewart pass. Then he followed the young man down the aisle, gently admonishing those who might be tempted to follow.

Bob Benson sat, looking properly distraught. He fidgeted and ran his fingers through his thinning hair. His wife tried to calm him.

Val and Ruby were sitting together. Val was doing her best to offer comfort.

The judge and Toulouse Gravelle were talking conspiratorially in a couple of seats that had been turned to face each other at the back of the coach.

Jack also noted a dark-haired young woman, sitting by herself, partway down the aisle. She alternated her attention between a well-thumbed Harry Potter book, the activities in the coach, and the scenery that was passing more slowly now that the alarm had been raised in the cab of the diesel that led the train.

Stewart had arrived at the door to the washroom. He stood staring at the lifeless body of Oscar Dempster.

The man sat on the floor with a rope around his neck. It was pulled tight and appeared to be deeply imbedded in the fleshy neck of the man from Simi Valley.

The other end of the rope appeared to have been looped over a coat hook that, before it had been torn away from the wall, had been attached approximately five-and-a-half feet above the floor. The hook now lay broken beside the slumped, fully-clothed, corpse.

Stewart searched for a pulse on Oscar's wrist. He shook his head. The victim's complexion appeared, to Jack, to be taking on a green tinge as he surveyed the dead man at close range.

"May I?" Jack asked, not waiting for permission, as he stooped, loosened the rope just enough, and felt for signs of life from the artery in Oscar's neck. He drew the same conclusion that Stewart obviously had.

He regretted having disturbed the evidence even that much.

If he had had any kind of pulse, it would have been worth it, he reasoned.

"You will want to make sure this site is secure," Jack said, in case the attendant was unsure what he wanted to do. "I think folks won't mind using the facilities in one of the other coaches until all this is settled."

Stewart nodded and struggled to his feet. He drew a tissue from the box that was attached to the wall by the sink and mopped his face.

Jack noticed that there was some water in the sink and a few drops of hand soap on the counter under the spout of the dispenser.

Stewart headed back to his station to make his

announcement, leaving Jack to close the door to what would now become the site of a police investigation.

The coach attendant had some duct tape in his supply cupboard, which Jack used to place a makeshift *X* across the doorway.

Chapter Five

"We'll be stopping at the next station," Stewart told Jack, when the private eye returned the roll of tape. "Someone has called ahead to let them know we will be there while this all gets sorted out. We've never had a suicide on one of our trains before. I'm not sure what the procedure is."

It's entirely possible you still haven't had a suicide, Jack thought.

"I'll do what I can to help," was what he said.

The train rumbled along at its reduced pace. It wasn't clear why that was the case. There was no way any amount of speed was going to wake up Oscar Dempster, as far as Jack could see.

Eventually the makeshift cortege arrived at a small

trackside shelter. The platform looked to be in much need of repair and there was no sign to identify the community to which it belonged.

The area where the station was located was surrounded by forest. A gravel road leading to the clearing was the only visible means of access. There was no indication that anything approaching civilization might be located nearby.

An ear piercing squeal of steel accompanied the application of brakes as the engineer brought the train to a stop.

The passengers listened as Stewart told them that, sadly, they would be here until the proper authorities had arrived to analyze the situation.

Up and down the train, each attendant was delivering a similar message but judiciously omitting the details of why it was necessary for the delay.

Jack looked around the coach. For the most part he saw only resignation on the faces of his fellow passengers.

Ruby Dempster was showing her obvious distress. Val was still doing her best to comfort the new widow.

Judge Marshall was standing in the vestibule at the front of the coach. Jack could see him talking on his cell phone.

Probably had a dinner engagement in Calgary tonight that has to be cancelled, he thought.

The young dark-haired girl was looking thoughtful as she read her book. Now and then she would look around the coach before returning to her reading. She saw Jack scanning the passengers and nodded to him, a faint smile on her lips.

I wonder if that means anything, Jack asked himself.

They waited for almost an hour before the authorities arrived. When the dust-covered, late model, black pickup came to rest by the platform, it soon became apparent that there was only one authority to deal with Oscar Dempster.

A woman and a man were visible in the cab. The woman did not get out.

The man wore a blue serge suit and a blue-and-gold striped tie. His shoes were polished to a fine sheen. They looked, to Jack, to be almost new.

The officer approached the trainman who, by now, had descended from the coach.

The new arrival reached into his pocket and produced, only briefly, a badge and identification.

The two men spoke. The trainman gestured emphatically at the coach and was apparently explaining what had been discovered earlier in the morning.

Finally, the officer mounted the stairs into the vestibule. He brushed past Judge Marshall, who was still standing there, though he had completed his phone call some time ago. Then he opened the door and walked into the passenger car.

The judge followed close behind and slipped by the officer, who had turned to address Stewart in a hushed voice.

After a few moments, the man with the badge turned to face an audience anxiously awaiting some indication that the delay, if not the horror of the morning's event, would soon come to an end.

"My name is Charles Roast. I am here to assure you that it is my intention to deal swiftly with this sad situation. I am sorry that your travel plans have been affected so tragically by the sudden passing of Mr. Dempster. My deep condolences to Mrs. Dempster over her loss.

"Unfortunately, in a case such as this, we need to keep moving along as quickly as possible. I have asked the trainman to start us moving again, as soon as the engineer can get clearance to proceed. We will take care of the gentleman in the washroom as best we can and will call for a coroner in Calgary. I will remain with you to ensure everything is properly handled. Enjoy the rest of your trip."

With that, he proceeded to the washroom and looked in. He shook his head, stooped briefly, apparently for a closer look, and stood again.

"Interesting," Jack whispered to Val, as he headed toward the officer at the end of the coach.

She looked up from her ministrations to Mrs. Dempster with a confused expression.

Jack looked out the window as he walked and saw the woman pull away from the platform in the official-looking pickup.

"My name's Jack," the private eye said to the man in

the blue suit. "Don't you think that this situation bears a little more attention?"

"You a cop?" the man asked.

"Used to be."

"Well, I still am. I know what I'm doing. This will all be taken care of in Calgary."

"Don't you think it should be dealt with here?" Jack asked.

"Look around out there," the blue suit replied. "We're in the middle of nowhere. There isn't a hospital or a police station for miles."

Jack had no reply, but his brain was going faster than the train at this point.

"Anything else?" Officer Roast asked, with a faint smile.

"Mind if I take a closer look at the victim?" Jack asked.

"Yeah, I do. That room's evidence. I don't want anyone moving Mr. Dempster until we get to the big city. Got that?"

Jack nodded.

"Look. I can see you have some real concerns about all this. Jack, is it?

"From what I can see, Mr. Dempster committed suicide in the washroom. I don't think there is much doubt of that."

"I don't think I'd be so quick to jump to that conclusion, Officer." Jack said. "Why would he choose to end his life in the middle of a vacation with his wife? Why here? Why now?"

"Why not here? I don't know. But let's assume the man is really depressed or has a terminal illness that he doesn't plan to fight. What better way to ensure that someone can't get him to medical help than to plan his own demise in the middle of nowhere?"

"There might be a doctor on board," Jack said. "He couldn't be sure of that."

"Okay, you've got me there. So, are you suggesting that Oscar Dempster died from something else?"

"I don't think it is beyond the realm of possibility. And, if he did, I think you need to be doing more than accompanying his body to the end of the line."

"That's all I intend to do. I'll leave the rest to someone else. Look, I'm all alone here. What do you want?" Roast said, and gave a shrug of the shoulders before walking away.

Jack watched after the retreating officer, who stopped briefly in the aisle to speak to Stewart and then pressed on into the next coach.

Jack needed to talk to Val, but she was still sitting with Ruby Dempster. It was apparent, though, that the older woman had calmed appreciably.

"Got a minute?" Jack asked his wife.

"Sure. What is it?" She looked up from where she was sitting and gave him one of those smiles that always made him glad they belonged to each other.

"Can I have a moment with you . . . alone?"

Val looked over at Mrs. Dempster, who was now

staring out the window as the forest began to move slowly past the window once more.

"I think she'll be all right for a few moments," Val whispered.

"Let's go up to our seats," Jack said, and took her hand.

They sat down together for the first time since the alarm had been raised earlier that morning.

"What's up?" Val asked. "I mean other than that poor man in the washroom."

"I need to do some investigating," Jack replied.

"Oh, Jack. We're on vacation," she said.

"Does this seem like a vacation to you?" he asked.

"Well . . ."—Val scanned the coach before returning her gaze to Jack's troubled-looking face—"I see what you mean."

"I've got to have a closer look at Mr. Dempster. And, I don't want to seem dramatic here, but I think there should be a little more dignity bestowed upon his body.

"Officer Roast seems unimpressed by the circumstances and is determined to leave things as they are until other authorities have a chance to look at him."

"You mean, he thinks this is a suicide? Has anyone moved Mr. Dempster?" Val asked.

"No. He's just the way we found him. I think he should be moved, at the very least. Any evidence there might be will be minimal, so I'm not concerned that we'll be making it any harder for the coroner."

"I think you're right, Jack. But I also think you

should get any evidence you can before you disturb anything. You've done this before. You know the drill."

Jack reflected on the numerous times as a police officer when he had been called to secure a sight and collect evidence. It had never been anything like the investigations folks had come to expect from watching too many episodes of the latest forensic drama on television.

"I'll talk to Stewart and get his support. Maybe you can help me with this. And then we can get Oscar moved to some place more appropriate."

"Wonderful way to spend our honeymoon, don't you think?" Valerie asked.

Jack went to talk to Stewart about his plan. The two men spoke for some time.

"I don't want to do anything that is going to get me, or the company, in any kind of trouble with the law," Stewart said, after Jack told him what he wanted to do.

"I can't make any promises, but I can assure you that both I and my wife, who is also a police officer, will take responsibility for everything that happens.

"I think Officer Roast is taking his responsibilities too seriously, or not seriously enough. I'm still trying to figure that one out. In any case, I think valuable time is being lost while we wait for our little caravan to arrive at the next oasis."

Stewart gave a weak smile.

"Okay. You can check around in there." He nodded toward the washroom at the end of the coach. "But please be careful. I don't want to lose my job."

"I assure you, Stewart, you will not lose your job. I'll make sure of that," Jack said.

Armed with cotton swabs and Ziploc bags from Stewart's supply cupboard, Jack retrieved Val from her seat and, together, the two of them proceeded to what was now the resting place of Oscar Dempster.

"Kind of an overuse of rope, don't you think?" Val asked, upon seeing the slumped and greying figure of Oscar Dempster.

The length of the rope between the hook and Oscar's neck was too great to have suspended him fully. If one assumed that the man had taken his own life, it wasn't immediately clear whether he had fastened it to the clasp and it had slipped from his weight before the hanger gave way, or whether Oscar had just been careful to make sure that he could not reach up to free himself, in case he had changed his mind.

"Well, at least he hasn't complained about the trip so far today," Jack said.

"That's humor far too dark for my liking," Val said.

"Sorry. Let's get to the task at hand. See anything noteworthy?"

"Save the rope," Val said.

"We'll let Oscar keep wearing it. I don't want to alter too many things, unless we have to," Jack replied.

"Let me get the camera," Val said. "We should photograph the scene before we move anything. And let's take pictures of anything that jumps out at us while we're doing this. I'm just sorry that all this will be interspersed with the pictures of the wedding reception and our tour of the city before we left."

Val left the washroom. She soon returned with the digital camera that Jack had used the day before to take photos of passing trains and sights outside the coach.

"Here ya go," she said. "It's a good thing you bought that new memory card. Knock yourself out."

There was very little for Jack to photograph, apart from the positioning of Oscar Dempster's dead body and a few close-ups of the rope around his neck. There were no other signs of trauma. It did not look as if Oscar Dempster had struggled at all.

"Are we agreed that the cause of death is strangulation?" Jack asked.

"Barring any evidence to the contrary, that would be my conclusion," Val replied. "You see anything else suspicious?"

"Can't say that I do. But I'm still a little concerned that all this looks just a little too clean. I'm not quite ready to conclude that old Oscar here, had had it with life to the point of wanting to end it. He enjoyed complaining too much. He vented his frustrations about absolutely everything. I don't believe he was suicidal."

"You suspect something else?" Val asked.

"The deadliest creature on earth," Jack replied.

Chapter Six

"Can I help?"

The question came from the doorway leading into the washroom where Jack and Val were leaning over the now-cold body of Oscar Dempster. The voice was definitely female. Jack turned to see who it was.

"Who are you?" he asked the dark-haired woman whom he had noticed before, sitting alone, toward the back of the coach reading Harry Potter.

"My name is Nadia. Nadia Vukasovich. I am a doctor. Well, almost a doctor. I'm just finishing my last year of studies."

"Well," Jack said, "you might be able to tell us a little more about our friend here. I'm afraid, though, that all the medical science in the world won't get him breathing again. Even I can tell that."

47

The soon-to-be Dr. Vukasovich was young looking and appeared very poised—a trait that Jack felt would certainly help when she was treating patients.

"You're certainly correct in your diagnosis of death as the presenting problem. It looks as if he hanged himself. But I'm not so sure. Have you moved anything?" she asked.

"Everything is exactly the way we found it," Jack said, feeling a slight sting to the ego. "I'm a cop. I know the importance of preserving evidence. We're hoping that we might be able to move Mr. Dempster after we've completed some preliminary investigation."

"Take it easy, my friend," the young woman said. "I'm not accusing you of anything. I'm just making sure my assumptions are correct. I'm new at this. I haven't learned how to cut corners yet."

She entered the small cubicle, making sure she did not disturb anything. She stooped to check the corpse propped up against the wall.

Jack moved to one side to let her perform her examination. Val stood against the wall and watched the young woman's gentle handling of someone who would not know the care he was receiving.

"Just as I thought," Nadia said, feeling around the neck of the late Mr. Dempster.

"And just what did you think?" Jack asked. His tone betrayed the twinge of pain he felt from this young woman's suggestion that he might not know how to handle a crime scene.

Jack still felt a deep pain when he remembered how he had been forced to leave his police work because of insinuations about his honesty and ability to do the work of keeping the peace. The drug bust that had turned bad had put him in the hospital and under suspicion of being in league with the bad guys. The physical pain had subsided long ago.

Though he had been exonerated and given an apology, the pain that the mistrust had caused still rested just below the surface. Emotional wounds were easy to open.

"Look, sir. If we're going to have to be together on this case, let alone this trip, we need to trust each other and use what expertise we have to deal with what I'm sure you'll admit is a rather horrific set of circumstances."

"I'm sorry. You're right," Jack said, and knew that she was.

"Call me Jack."

"Okay, Jack. What I thought was that, this man . . . what's his name . . . Dempster? Mr. Dempster probably did die from hanging. I don't suspect that anyone else had a hand in bringing about his demise. But I don't think it was a quick death either."

"What makes you say that?" Jack asked.

"Let me do a little more checking here, and I'll be able to give you a clearer picture."

Nadia returned to her examination. It was clear that she was still using a gentle touch on her patient, in spite of his evident insensibility to what she was doing.

Jack stepped into the aisle outside the lavatory. He

noticed that inquisitive passengers would walk by, from time to time, and give a sideways glance into the washroom.

Jack spoke quietly to Stewart, urging that some refreshments might be advisable. With table trays down, the passengers would have just one more barrier to their milling about and hindering what had become a makeshift investigation. If what Nadia had said was true, everything would be sorted out soon enough. But Jack was suspicious that there was more to the situation than met the eye.

Valerie had left Nadia to her examination and was sitting beside Ruby Dempster, doing her very best to calm the woman who had become agitated again, in the young woman's absence.

Val had counseled with those who were grieving before. In her vocation as a police officer she had been called upon to help, especially on those occasions when there was the need for a calming female voice.

Today she was having only moderate success.

Ruby Dempster was looking frail and colorless. She had chewed off the bright-red lipstick, run her fingers through her hair too many times for it to be possible to tame it again without some serious professional help, and had lost the healthy glow that judiciously applied makeup had afforded her earlier in the day.

The Widow Dempster dabbed at her eyes with a lace hanky, now damp with tears and discolored by the camouflage that had been transferred from her face.

"Why would he do such a thing? Why would my Oscar hang himself? What could have been wrong? Oh, I'm so confused. I don't know what to think. Oh dear, what am I going to do now? Oh, Oscar, you beast. How could you leave me like this?"

"Now, Mrs. Dempster—Ruby. Don't get yourself all worked up like this," Val said. "I'm sure there are answers to all your questions. I'm sure your husband loved you dearly. I can't answer your questions right now, but I'm sure we will all get some answers soon. I'll do my best to take care of you in the meantime. Would you like some tea?"

The truth was that Valerie did not know, for sure, that the answers Ruby would get would be at all satisfying to the elderly woman. Like the woman sitting beside her, she assumed that Oscar had been so overcome with the cares of this life that he had decided to end it all. So far, there was no evidence to the contrary.

But, why here? she wondered.

It was a question that would occupy many minds before the *Last Spike Special* arrived at its final destination. Indeed, it was a question that threatened to keep the passengers and crew on the train for some time after it had reached its final destination.

"Can I speak to you for a moment?"

Nadia was standing in the doorway to the washroom, motioning Jack to step inside.

"What is it? Did you find something?" Jack asked.

"Yeah, I think I have. I think that, maybe, this is more than just a suicide," she said in a whisper.

"Okay. What have you got?" Jack asked.

"Well, it starts with what I don't have," the young doctor-to-be said. "I checked around his neck and there are no broken vertebrae so he would have had to strangle to death. The bruising that we see there is another indication that he asphyxiated. Not a pleasant thing. He would have struggled to breathe, in spite of his intentions, if he was taking his own life. I see no signs of that."

"You're suggesting that there was something else that killed him?" Jack asked.

"Well, to really get a definitive answer, you'd need to do an autopsy. I'm not able to do that, first off. And then, as you can plainly see, we don't have the facilities. But I can give you a preliminary theory and some hard evidence to get you started," Nadia said.

"I'm listening."

"He strangled to death."

"But you said . . ."

"Let me finish."

"Sorry," Jack said, and waited for the young woman to continue.

"He strangled to death, but he was unconscious when it happened. That's why there are no signs of struggle, and very few abrasions on his neck. Besides that, he is more livid than I might expect had he been hanged with his full weight on the end of the rope."

She indicated to pinpoint-size blood spots on the man's bloated face.

"While petechial hemorrhages can be present in some natural deaths, the presence of the rope sort of rules that out. He strangled, or was strangled."

"What is your theory about what happened," Jack asked.

"Someone made sure he lost consciousness in a hurry. I'll get to that in a moment. Then they looped the rope around his neck and bent his knees to tighten the knot. After that, it was an easy task to pull his feet forward so he would hang.

"Problem is, that clothes hook on the wall presented two dilemmas. First, it is small. The diameter of the rope made it almost impossible to make a secure knot that would keep it from slipping. Thus, the slack. Then these things are secured to the wall by two screws, at most. The material used for the wall is some sort of composite with a plastic covering. It is durable enough for day-to-day use, but won't hold a man the size of Mr. Dempster with just two wood screws. So we've got a broken hook that's been pulled out of the wall."

"You said someone made him lose consciousness before he strangled," Jack said. "Care to explain?"

"I was concerned by the lack of evidence of a real hanging, so I took a closer look at his neck. By the way, whoever did this, had to tighten the knot manually. They stood beside him and pulled. Not a pleasant thing to think about.

"Anyway, as I was examining Mr. Dempster's neck, I found this."

With that, she leaned the body forward and pointed to a spot in the back just below the man's collar.

"I must be blind," Jack said. "I must confess, I don't see anything."

"I didn't either, at first," Nadia said. "Look a little closer. Do you see those marks?"

"You mean those two red spots. Not vampires, I hope."

"Shall we try to keep serious here?" she asked.

"Sorry. What is it?" Jack asked.

"Probes."

Jack resisted the urge to ask if it was a failed alien abduction and decided to listen.

Nadia continued. "I am willing to bet that those marks were left by some sort of electrical device. It's like a cattle prod, only smaller. We have them in my country. Some police use them. There are smaller ones for personal protection. Taser is the brand name."

"Well, the police use Taser electronic control devices—ECD for short—to subdue people who are violent or uncooperative," Jack offered. "Don't hear of too many regular folks having one, though."

"Oh. Okay. So, it's the same as in my home country, Argentina."

"I would have thought you were European, with a name like Nadia Vukasovich."

"Very good. I mean, most people don't remember my last name, let alone pronounce it correctly the first time. Actually, my grandparents come from Italy and Yugoslavia. But my parents live in Argentina. I'm named after a famous Romanian Olympic gymnast."

"Sorry to sidetrack you. You were saying that you thought the marks came from some kind of electroshock device," Jack said.

"I'm making that assumption. Those little marks are burns. I don't believe there is anything else that would leave that sort of 'fingerprint' on the skin. I think someone immobilized Mr. Dempster first, and then tried to hang him. It just didn't work out the way it was planned."

"Goes to show you, you should always make sure you have the right tools for the job, I guess," Jack said.

"You have a truly strange sense of humor, Jack."

"It comes from having to deal with a lot of tragic circumstances, I guess. Compensation."

"In any case," Nadia continued, "that's what I conclude from my observations. I can't speak for the coroner, or those who do this on a regular basis."

"How do you know about Taser?" Jack asked. "Doesn't sound like something they would talk about in medical school."

"The proper generic term is *electroshock device* or *electronic control device*. There are all sorts of tools used to control people or subdue them. Taser is one of the companies you read about most. The police use their products. Do you know what it stands for?" Nadia asked, smiling.

"Can't say that I do," Jack replied.

"Thomas A. Swift's Electric Rifle."

"You're just a fount of knowledge."

"I needed to get something like that for myself. A young woman on the streets of the city at night can be a target for a lot of things," she said.

"Kind of bulky to be carrying."

"Not at all. A consumer version is available that is about the size of a cell phone. They even make them in designer colors. Packs a walloping fifty-thousand volts. A shock like that would really get someone's attention."

"So, you think someone smuggled one on the train?" Jack asked.

"Easy to do. Easy to get rid of."

"So, it's as I suspected," Jack said. "Someone wanted this man dead."

"Yeah. Go figure. Now, who might he have offended lately? You've got a whole coachload of suspects, myself included. And, my friend, what about you? I understand you fancy yourself as some sort of private eye."

"I'll have to admit, the guy wasn't making too many fast friends yesterday. I'm not sure that he was obnoxious enough to make someone snap, though."

"That's not my area of expertise," Nadia said. "You've got about seven hours before we arrive in Calgary. Better start investigating. I gather the guy in the suit is just going to enjoy the ride until we get there."

"Thanks for your help. I guess I know what my assignment is," Jack replied. "Now, let's see if we can get this poor man moved to a better place."

"Oh, I think he's already in a better place," the student doctor replied, with a broad smile.

"I see my sense of humor is rubbing off," Jack said. "I guess I'd better go speak to the cop who got on a while ago."

Jack got his chance sooner than he had expected.

"And just what do you two think you're doing?"

The booming voice betrayed deep anger. It belonged to Charles Roast. One look at his face was enough to convince Jack that there would need to be some fast talking.

"Oh! Hi, officer. I've been talking to the coach attendant about Mr. Dempster here. He sort of felt it best if we moved the body to another coach, out of sight of the passengers.

"Look. I've done this sort of stuff before. I'm a cop too. I know what to look for. There is no other evidence in here to be disturbed, as far as I can see. You said yourself that this was a suicide."

A cloud crossed Roast's face momentarily. Jack wasn't sure if it was suspicion, doubt, or something else.

Nadia looked as if she was going to speak, but Jack gave her a quick glance that served its purpose. She returned a knowing nod.

Jack continued, "It's warm in here. The air conditioning doesn't quite compensate for the sun coming through that frosted window. Mr. Dempster might make his presence felt in more ways than one if we don't get him to cooler quarters.

"If you haven't finished your investigation, it is certainly your prerogative to close yourself in with Mr. Dempster until you're done. I just thought it best if the rest of these folks didn't have to share your experience."

The policeman gave the suggestion some thought before taking matters into his own hands.

"Let's, you and me, pack everything together carefully and get some of those blankets from the overhead racks," Roast said. "Try not to disturb things too much. We can take him somewhere where there aren't too many people. Any suggestions?"

"Stewart says the next coach has a place that is used by the crew. It has a number of rooms that used to be private accommodations for transcontinental travel. We can probably use one of those."

"Okay. Let's do that," Roast agreed. "And when we're done, stay away from the body. Got that?"

"We'll ask them to turn up the AC in the room so that Mr. D. won't suffer too many effects of the heat," Jack said as he escorted Nadia out of the washroom and then headed down the aisle to arrange the transfer with Stewart.

Chapter Seven

With Stewart's help, Jack managed to bundle Oscar Dempster in railway blankets. The trainman and an attendant from another coach helped move the dead man's body into the adjoining car, where they placed it in an unused cabin.

Roast had left the coach after agreeing to the transfer.

After turning up the air conditioning as high as it would go, the trainman locked the door and pocketed the key.

Jack thanked everyone for their assistance and followed Stewart back into their coach.

As he went, he scanned the rows of seats. He wasn't sure what he was expecting to see. He knew from experience that guilty people don't always look guilty, and those that do are often innocent.

He saw Nadia was back in her seat and reading about the boy wizard again. He walked down the aisle to where she was.

"Thanks for your help. You've confirmed what I suspected ever since the beginning of this nasty business. I guess that I've got my work cut out for me. Can I call on you again, if I need your expertise?"

Looking up from her book, Nadia replied, "I'm no expert, but I'll do what I can, Jack. Good luck with your investigation."

"Thanks. I think I'll need all the luck I can find. By the way, so far only you and I know about what we found. I'd like to keep it that way."

"I'll just sit and read my book," Nadia said. "I don't know anything." She smiled at Jack.

Valerie was still sitting with Ruby Dempster. The woman appeared noticeably calmer. She had obviously managed to get to the neighboring coach. Her makeup had been reapplied, and some semblance of organization had returned to her hair.

Jack caught his wife's attention, and they returned to their seat together.

"I've been talking to that young woman toward the back. Nadia's her name."

"Yeah, I noticed." Valerie said. Her voice hinted at being upset with her husband.

"Hey, look," Jack said. "We were just investigating the situation with Mr. D. That's all."

"Oh, I know, Jack. It's just that this is our honeymoon and look how it's turning out. Besides," she said, with a hint of a smile, "I thought I was your sidekick."

"You are and always will be, Dr. Watson," he replied. Then he took her face between his hands and kissed her on the forehead.

"You looked a little preoccupied with other things," he continued with a nod toward the seat just behind them that held Mrs. Dempster. "I didn't want to distract you from an equally valuable task."

"Oh, you. You always were a sweet talker, Jack Elton." Valerie smiled at her husband and gave his hand a reassuring squeeze. "Just remember. I'm here for you."

"Fear not, young lady. I will not forget you, though coaches and walls do separate us. But, now, I must away. Duty calls."

"Silly man," Valerie said as Jack headed down the coach to talk with Stewart once again. Then she returned to her post beside Ruby. The older woman noticed her return and patted the young woman's hand.

"Mind if we have a little chat, Stewart?"

The man looked at his watch before replying.

"Sure. I've got a few minutes before I have to start organizing a snack for you folks. Let's sit down for a minute. It's a good excuse to get off my feet for a bit."

"Let's talk about this job of yours. I'm fascinated with trains. Maybe you can help me understand how this particular operation works."

"Glad to help, if I can. I love this job. This is the best summer work I've ever had."

"I was just wondering," Jack said, "with all the concerns about terrorism and violence these days, are there any special precautions you have to take?"

"Well, Mr. Elton, we have yet to have a train hijacked to the Middle East. Sorry, I couldn't resist. Actually, we do have safety measures in place. Not so much to deal with terrorists, but sometimes you get a passenger who is so unruly that special steps are necessary."

"Any special equipment like . . . oh, I don't know. How about one of those electroshock thingies. I had one when I was on the police force."

"Can't say," Stewart replied.

"You don't know?" Jack asked, amazed.

"No. I can't say. I mean I'm not permitted to tell you what we might, or might not, have.

"Not even me?" Jack asked.

"Not even you." Stewart replied. "You seem to know what you are doing, but I only have your word for it that you are a real investigator."

Jack could tell he meant it. He was regretting that he had left his police department credentials back home.

"Let's change the subject," Jack said. "I just was wondering about your thoughts on what happened this morning."

"Well, I think it's terrible. What sorts of thoughts go through a person's mind that would make them want to end their lives that way? I mean, gee, we all have bad days, but I've never thought of dealing with them like that."

The attendant had what appeared to be a genuine look of distress on his young face.

"He sure seemed upset about a lot of things, though," Jack said. "Gave you a pretty rough time of it. I guess he won't be able to do that anymore."

"What are you suggesting?" Stewart asked, his voice rising in both pitch and volume. "You have no right . . ."

"You've got to admit, Oscar Dempster was not your best customer," Jack said, cocking his head to one side and smiling.

"Mr. Elton, let me tell you, I've had far worse guests than Mr. Dempster on my coach. On a scale of one to ten, he was down at the bottom of the list. We're taught that the customer is always right, and I live by that motto. I've had folks get on this train, though, who thought they should get absolutely everything they ask for. They want fine dining. They want to ride in the ob-servation coach. Some have even demanded to ride in the engine. Those are the folks who I would happily have throttled with my bare hands.

"No. I'm sorry to see Mr. Dempster go like that. He shouldn't have done that to himself."

"Stewart, thanks for putting my mind at ease," Jack said, finally. "I'm going to be talking to some of the passengers this afternoon. I don't know what may come of it but I suspect that there is a murderer on board. I'm convinced it's not you, and I could use your help.

"Officer Roast might think otherwise. I haven't consulted with him. In fact I have not shared my suspicions with him. I'm going to ask you to keep it to yourself for now. Can you do that for me?"

"Well, that is terrifying news, Mr. Elton."

"Call me Jack."

"Okay, Jack. Yes. Certainly. I'll do all I can to help. And I won't mention what you've told me to anyone. But why not—"

Jack held up a cautioning hand.

"Not even the other staff, please."

The coach attendant nodded his assent.

Jack headed off to what was promising to be a tiring day. He was regretting the previous evening's insomnia. Even in death, Oscar Dempster managed to have a negative impact on the lives of people he had only just met.

Chapter Eight

"**W**ell, hi there, young fella. How's it going for you today?"

Judge William Marshall had a broad smile on his face as he greeted Jack.

"Mind if I sit down for a moment?" Jack asked. "I didn't get much sleep last night. Strange bed. Hot weather. You know how it is."

"Can't say that I do. How is it?" The older man didn't wait for an answer. He just threw back his head and laughed his characteristic laugh.

"Let's just say I'm feeling a little tired today," Jack replied. "Not really able to focus on all the new things we're seeing. Of course, that poor man dying like that sure puts a cloud in the sky."

"Well, I suppose it all depends on how ya look at it,"

the judge said. "T'would appear that the man just didn't want to keep on living. Sometimes we get to feeling that we're no earthly good. That's not to say that he's going to be any heavenly good either, I suppose. As it is, neither you nor I can bring him back from wherever he is, so there's no use trying. Too bad he had to go that way, though. Could have been otherwise, if he'd made up his mind about it."

"I suppose you're right. If he'd only taken some time to talk out his frustrations, you think that might have made a difference?" Jack asked.

"Let me tell you, son, I've sat on the bench for many years now. I've seen people come and go. I've even had folks come before me again and again. And over and over, I put them away to think about what they've done. And do you think they learn their lesson? Do you think they change their ways? No, siree, they don't. We give them counseling. We put them on parole and give them a professional to refer to, and it just doesn't seem to help, most of the time."

"That must frustrate you," Jack suggested.

"I liked it better when we could put them out of their misery, if you know what I mean."

"I know you developed quite a reputation for yourself in younger years. I would imagine that you had your share of enemies because of that," Jack said.

"I think some of 'em agreed with me but were afraid to come right out and say it. I mean opponents to hanging. The criminals never agreed."

Again the Judge's laugh echoed up and down the car.

"You were having a rather animated debate with Mr. Gravelle when I left the two of you last night. How did that go?"

"Old Luce and I don't agree on a lot of things. He presents himself as a pacifist. It's good for his political career most of the time. But, I'll tell you, he was some bent out of shape about Dempster. Those two must have had some sort of real set-to yesterday, before we stopped for the night. Gravelle was fit to be tied. If the guy hadn't died already, Luce probably would have strangled him himself."

"Interesting observation, Judge Marshall," Jack said. "You really think he would be capable of something like that? I mean, he looks to be such a calm sort of guy."

"Appearances can be deceiving," the judge said.

"You got that right," Jack replied. "Well, I guess we might as well enjoy the rest of the trip. Nothing to do before we get to the end and the coroner gets to confirm the cause of death."

"Yep," the jurist said, putting his clasped hands behind his head, leaning back, and gazing out at the passing countryside.

The train was passing along one side of a deep gorge that had been cut into the rock by the river below. As the sun rose higher in the sky, its rays warmed the interior of the shiny coaches. The soft breeze of the air conditioning kept the passengers isolated from what the weather forecasters had predicted would be a day of scorching heat.

Stewart had started down the aisle with a cart loaded with mid-morning snacks.

Jack watched as, one by one, his coach mates stared into the cart and selected single-serving bags of cookies, pretzels, or chips. Stewart had hot and cold beverages to offer as well.

Jack appeared to get so caught up in his observations that the wagon was soon beside where he and the judge were sitting.

Blocked in as he now was, Jack turned toward William Marshall, who had closed his eyes and appeared to be happily soaking up the sun's rays.

"Since I'm here, mind if I stay a while longer? I'd like to hear more about your life on the bench and what sort of things you did when you weren't judging cases."

"Always happy to talk about myself, son. I find most people are, though they're afraid to admit it. Glad to have the company. I think Gravelle and I covered all the bases we care to last night. He's off in the vestibule watching mile markers go by or something. Only met him yesterday. I guess they figured two guys traveling solo would be good to put together. They probably figured we'd either find something to talk about or would just be happy to ignore each other for most of the trip. I guess we're doing both."

"I've heard a lot about your successes," Jack said. "Are there any cases that stand out in your mind that you'd like to be remembered for?"

The judge threw back his head and gave a loud and long rendition of his trademark laugh.

"I appreciate your interest, sonny," he said, when he had finally calmed enough to speak. "I've been having a grand time on this trip. Haven't laughed so much in years."

"I don't suppose there is much cause for laughter in the midst of a trial for murder," Jack said.

"You're right, there," came the reply. "Although, I've had my share of funny situations, in spite of all that."

"Really?"

"I'll be the first to admit that lawyers get a bad rap most of the time. But as a judge, I've had to listen to some pretty bad lawyering. I remember one case where we had a defense lawyer who decided to press the limits of credibility by questioning whether the pathologist had done everything to determine that the victim was dead."

"Sounds a little risky, after the fact," Jack said.

"As I remember it, the guy asked one of our best pathologists if he had bothered to check for a pulse. This is in the autopsy room, mind you. The doc says no. 'Well, did you listen to his heart,' Mr. Wise Lawyer asks. Same reply.

"I'm starting to get a little crazy about this time, but I hold my peace. I wanna see where this thing is going."

"What happened?" Jack asked.

"Well, he's not through. Figures he'll move in for the kill. Sorry, bad choice of words. Anyway, he asks the doctor if he bothered to check for breathing. Doc says no and gives the guy a strange look. Couldn't really blame him.

" 'So you weren't absolutely sure the man was dead. And yet you signed the death certificate,' the guy says, and then stands back, with his hands on his hips and tries to look properly hurt by the pathologist's oversight."

Jack was sitting on the edge of the seat, waiting for what he knew was going to be a fitting end to the judge's story.

"You know what that doctor said? You won't believe it when I tell you." Judge Marshall let out a howl of laughter. "He looks Mr. Smarty Pants square in the eye and says, 'Well, sir, I had the man's brain sitting in a stainless basin on the table, but I guess it's possible the guy is out practicing law somewhere today.' "

Judge William Marshall lost whatever composure remained at this point. The sound of his overjoy could be heard up and down the coach.

Jack began to feel a certain embarrassment for having been the catalyst for this outburst.

"Oh, forgive me, son," the judge finally said. "I've been living under a certain amount of tension lately. It's good to get that out."

"Did that really happen?" Jack asked, incredulous.

"Maybe it did. Maybe it didn't. Tell ya the truth. If it did happen, it wasn't in my courtroom. But it's mighty funny. Coulda happened, I suppose. I saw you smile."

"It's a good story, that's for sure. Got any real stories?"

"Aw, Jack. Am I a disappointment to you? I'll try to do better."

Jack sat back, listening.

"Okay, I'll be serious. This one's the truth. And not one bit funny.

"There was a case I adjudicated, where a man was brought up on a manslaughter charge. He'd been under the influence, to say the least, one evening. Got into a big, powerful car and decided to test the acceleration down the middle of the main drag in a little town in Ontario. The guy was crazy. He was, from all accounts, weaving all over the place. Anyway, he loses control, climbs onto the sidewalk, and takes out three of four members of one family. They were out for a walk. Weren't hurting anyone. Minding their own business and this guy kills Mom, Dad, and a six-year-old girl. Leaves only the teenaged son."

"That's tragic," Jack said.

"What's more tragic," the judge said, "was that the guy gets off on a technicality. He makes a deal to plead guilty, get counseling, and stay away from alcohol. In exchange, he gets a few nights in jail, at taxpayers' expense, and then returns to live his happy little life. All he has to do is sit with someone who's paid to listen for an hour a week. He gets to complain about how tough life has treated him and gets told that life can be meaningful without the use of alcohol."

"What happened?" Jack asked.

"Nothing much for the court to do. The Crown

Counsel agreed to the terms. They dropped the manslaughter charge and made it reckless driving, or some such thing, and put the guy on parole. He eventually moved away."

"That's really sad," Jack said.

"Yeah," the judge replied. "The boy who lost his family was old enough to know what was happening and resolved to do something about that sort of thing. Became a cop. A good one from what I hear."

"Maybe some good will come of all this after all," Jack said.

Judge Marshall nodded.

"What about your other cases?" Jack asked.

"I try real hard not to think about my own stuff, son. It's too depressing. Maybe I'll tell you before the trip is over."

By now, Stewart had completed his trip to the end of the aisle and had returned to the small cubicle that housed his daily supplies. He had stowed his cart and was reviewing his script for the afternoon's points of interest.

Jack knew that his own mind would be unable to focus on anything that was said. He wondered how true that might be for others who had shared the sad events of the morning. He assumed, too, that someone would have their mind occupied with thoughts of how to escape discovery or prosecution. He was convinced that someone had put an end to Oscar Dempster and that the individual was still on the train.

Jack was working feverishly to determine who that individual might be.

He excused himself, slipped out of the seat next to Judge Marshall, and returned to his own place.

Val was sitting alone again.

In other seats were couples or small groups traveling together who Jack judged to be unremarkable in outward appearance but whom, he knew, could be successfully hiding homicidal tendencies.

Chapter Nine

"I'm getting weary, Jack."

Val was looking drained of most of her energy. Her hair had become untidy, and the light had gone from her eyes.

"I'm sorry, honey," Jack said. "Can I do anything to help?"

Val lowered her voice to answer her husband.

"Mrs. Dempster is just so upset. I mean, that is to be expected, but there just seems to be nothing I can say that seems to help. She cries. She questions. She's so concerned about what the future holds for her. Mr. Dempster was the one who took care of everything. In fact, from what she said, it seems as if he didn't let her do anything on her own and when she did, he'd chew her out for even trying. I know I should

74

show more compassion but, gosh, I'm supposed to be on holiday."

"Well, Mrs. Elton, if it's any consolation, we'll be at our destination in seven or eight more hours, depending on the traffic."

"What traffic? This isn't the highway. Are you teasing me?"

"Not exactly. This train isn't part of the transcontinental system. It's running on borrowed tracks, so to speak. If there is a freight, or if we meet one of the scheduled passenger trains, we're going to have to sit on a siding and let them pass. That's why all the literature about our trip says we are estimated to arrive at such and such a time. We could arrive any time between six and seven or later, if we get sidetracked. And I do mean that in the literal sense."

"Well, it's tiring," Val said, "and I'm feeling bad that I'm feeling this way. I've dealt with grief before. I do it all the time on the force."

"Yes, but you have the opportunity to leave after you've done your job. Where are you going to go while you're on here?" He made a sweeping gesture.

"I see what you mean. I'm sorry."

She smiled.

"I'm sorry too," Jack said. "I haven't been much company for you today. I'll try to make it up to you once we get to the city. We can be tourists for awhile and, hopefully, forget all this."

"I doubt that we'll ever be able to forget, Jack. But I

know what you mean. Where shall we go? Why do you have that look on your face?"

"I guess I'm not ready to make plans just yet. I've got some other things that need my attention right now. I wish Officer Roast hadn't decided to run off to first class before carrying out his duty. He seems convinced that Oscar Dempster did himself in. I know that's not the case. And I'm a little suspicious of the guy.

"I would have thought that he would, at least, care enough to take the initiative to have the poor man's body relocated. He only gave it a cursory glance, told me to go ahead, and then headed off to enjoy the rest of his trip. He appears to think his only responsibility is as some sort of escort. And he's not even doing that very well.

"Maybe it's just me. We'll see."

"I'm sure my big, brave detective will get this case solved before too long. I have faith in you," Val said.

"Thanks. I wish I had your confidence," Jack said. "Mind if I have a chat with your friend one seat back?"

"Go for it. I think I'm going to close my eyes for a while. Call me if you need me."

A thin voice called over Jack's shoulder, "Oh, Valerie. Can you come back here for a moment?"

"Mrs. Dempster, I'll come and talk to you, if you don't mind," Jack said, and slid out of his seat.

"You're both so kind, you and Valerie," Ruby said. "This is so hard. I don't know what I'll do. Oscar was such a support to me. Now I'm all alone."

Tears were welling up in her eyes again.

"Mrs. Dempster, I'd like to ask you a few questions," Jack said.

"Oh, young man, call me Ruby, please. I don't know now. Should I still be Mrs. Dempster, now that Oscar is. . . . Oh dear, I don't even want to say the word."

"Yes, Mrs. Dempster—Ruby—you should still use that name.

"Tell me about you and Oscar. How long have you been married?"

"Well, I'm not sure that I can, right now. I'm just so upset. But you look like such a nice young man, and I really need someone to talk to. You know, since this morning, my mind has been so full of memories. It's not quite like what they say."

"How do you mean, Mrs. Dem . . . I mean Ruby?"

"Well they say that when you, you know . . . I just can't use that word. When you see the end coming, your life flashes before you."

Jack nodded his encouragement.

"Well, I've been the one who has seen Oscar's life, and mine too, flash before me since this morning. There is so much that is coming back.

"Your Valerie has been such a help today. But I'm afraid I may tire her out. She needs a rest from this."

"Take your time," Jack said. "I promise I'm a good listener."

Let me see," the woman began, and started counting

on her fingers. "We got married when I was seventeen. Oscar had to ask my father for my hand. It was so cute watching him try to talk to Dad.

"My parents knew a proposal was coming. They could read the signs. We were so in love. Dad decided that he would make Oscar sweat a little before agreeing to let him marry me. Truth was, they were glad that someone else was going to be responsible for me. They didn't have a lot of money, and Oscar was starting out in business. They saw him as a pretty good catch, I guess.

"Now, where was I? Oh yes. I was seventeen when he proposed. I suppose Oscar must have been about twenty-one by then. Yes, I'm sure of it, he was twenty-one. We got married just before my eighteenth birthday and I turned sixty-six last month. My, how the time flies. So we've been married for, let's see, forty-nine years. That's right. It was going to be our fiftieth anniversary next year. Oh, dear."

A definite tremor was entering into her voice again. Jack decided to press on.

"Were they happy years, Ruby? I mean, every marriage has its ups and downs, but would you say that, for the most part, it was a happy marriage?"

"Oh, my, yes. It was mostly good. Well, except for when Oscar got angry. I'd do some silly thing, and he'd get mad and yell. And sometimes he'd get physical. He'd bloodied my nose a couple of times. Mind you, that was only when he'd been drinking too much. Mostly, though, he'd just talk real loud and tell me that I was useless. He'd sometimes say he was sorry he ever married me, but I knew he really didn't mean it."

"That must have made you a little angry at times, though," Jack said.

"Certainly," she said, looking right at Jack. "There were times I was ready to strangle him with my bare hands."

Suddenly a look of horror came over the woman's face.

"Oh," she gasped. "I can't believe I just said that. You must think I'm awful."

"No. I think that's understandable," Jack said, though he wondered if frustration might finally have gotten the best of her, considering how irritating the man had been the day before.

"Can you think of any reason why he might have wanted to take his own life?" Jack asked.

"Can't think of a one," she replied. "He was as happy as a lark. Mind you, he often seemed happiest when he was making things difficult for others. I don't know if you'd noticed, in the short time you had to see him."

Jack thought it best not to answer. Ruby seemed to have had motive enough. But, did she have the means or the opportunity?

If I'd known this was going to happen, I could have kept a closer eye on everyone earlier this morning, he thought, and then realized how silly the sentiment truly was. Val would have laughed. But he wasn't going to tell her.

Ruby was looking at him and asking a question. Jack snapped out of his reverie.

"I'm sorry. What was that?" he asked.

"I was just wondering where that nice police officer went to. The one who got on back there. Officer Roast. I wanted to ask him a question. No matter. It wasn't that important.

"Now, I think you should get back to your lovely new wife. She's looking a little distressed. I don't know if you'd noticed."

Jack smiled.

"Thank you. I'll do just that. It's been nice talking to you. Thanks for answering my questions. And Ruby, I'm really sorry about Oscar."

"You're too kind," she replied, and dabbed her eyes with her hankie.

Jack stood and returned to the empty seat beside Valerie.

"Have a good chat?" she asked.

"Informative. Troubling. All that and more," he said. "She's on my suspect list for now. Do you think she could have killed her husband?"

"Keep your voice down. She'll hear you. And, yes, she could have. Anger can give you a lot of strength in the heat of the moment. You think she might have done it? She seems so broken up by all this."

"Maybe she's overcome with grief at the realization

of what she's done. She was so angry, maybe she couldn't wait for their fiftieth anniversary."

"Wow! They were married almost fifty years? You think we'll last that long, Jack?"

"Not if we have to keep on doing this kind of stuff on what is supposed to be a vacation," Jack said, smiling.

"Of course we will," he added. "We're so in love, it will last a hundred years or more."

"Silly man," Val said, and giggled for the first time that day.

Chapter Ten

"Hello, my friend. Sit down. Tell me how your morning is going so far."

Nadia Vukasovich, the medical student from Argentina, had been reading her Harry Potter book when Jack had walked back to where she was sitting.

"Are you enjoying the story?" he asked as he took a seat.

"Oh, yes. I want to read them all. I began reading the series when I was a teenager. Of course, I read the Spanish version. I've read this one before, but not in English. I still have a few problems understanding the language. But, since I know what is supposed to happen, I can figure out the tough words."

She closed the book.

"Now, Jack Elton, tell me what is happening. I really want to know."

"Well, soon-to-be-doctor Vukasovich, I've got a few suspects. But first I've got a few questions. Mind if I ask you for some clarification, just so we both understand where we stand?"

Nadia looked hurt.

"You don't trust me," she said, and stuck out her lower lip in a feigned pout.

"At this point, I can't afford to trust anyone. I'm sorry if it offends you, but I've got to exercise what we call due diligence. Trust me, it will only hurt for a little while, and then it will all be over."

She smiled.

"You'd make a good doctor. That's what we tell our young patients when we have to give them a needle. Okay, I'll trust you. But I want a Mickey Mouse bandage."

"Believe me. I won't leave any marks," Jack said, laughing.

"All right. I'm ready," Nadia said, and looked up at him with large brown eyes.

"Ever heard of Oscar Dempster before this trip?"

"I wouldn't have known who he was, if you hadn't told me. I can't say that I've had a lot of contact with anyone on the train. I'm just on a break from school. I like Canada. I was here some years ago as an exchange student and resolved, before I left, that I would come back to see some more of it. And here I am. But I haven't been here for over ten years. I hadn't met anyone in this coach until I boarded yesterday."

"Well, now you know me and Val and Mrs. Dempster, I guess," Jack said. "What was your opinion of Oscar?"

"He was a very—how should I say this—forceful man. Loud too. I don't think I would have grown to like him. But I need to add that I'm sorry he's dead. He didn't deserve to go that way."

"And you're convinced that 'that way' was at the hands of another?"

"I can't see it having happened any other way," Nadia replied. "I believe he was incapacitated by someone with an electroshock device. He was strangled, and a feeble attempt at making it look like suicide was made."

"I guess what concerns me is that you know so much about this process. Want to set my mind at ease?"

"I don't know if I can," she said. "I do know a lot about this stuff from my medical studies and, I hate to say it, from personal experience. I won't pretend to be dumb just to deflect any lingering doubts you might have. You'll have to come to your own conclusions. You've only got a short time to do that, so you'd better get on with your questions."

"I'm listening," Jack said. "I didn't mean to offend you."

"As I said, I have been studying medicine for ten years now. All this information is kind of fresh in my mind. So, when you ask for an opinion, I can feed back a whole library full of information about what makes a person dead. Give me time. I'm sure I won't be such a ready fountain of knowledge. All I can tell you is I know what to look for. I know what physical things I need to check to start making a diagnosis. Oscar Dempster was strangled to death. The evidence points to that. Any doctor or pathologist would tell you the same thing."

"You spoke about personal experience," Jack said.

"Yeah. Well, that has to do with why I know so much about the electroshock thing. That comes from necessity."

Jack raised his eyebrows and nodded in an "okay, go on" gesture.

"My dad used to work at a gas station. One night some really bad men came in with guns and threatened to kill him unless he turned over all the money in the till."

"What happened?" Jack asked.

"What would you have done? He opened the drawer and gave them all his money. Fortunately, they left without causing him any physical harm. But he decided that he should sell the business and look for a safer place to live too. We moved to another town. Now he and my mother run a little coffee shop."

"But they are still in danger from thieves," Jack said.

"That's true. But now my father has protection behind the counter. He's never played baseball, but he owns a very fine Louisville Slugger. And he has a stun gun in the cash drawer. He's taken training, so he knows how to use it.

"When I was a teenager, he wanted to protect me as best he could, so he sent me to take a self-defense course. You don't want to meet up with me when I'm in a bad mood, if you know what I mean."

Jack knew. He had taken the training himself, when he had joined the police force. He could still remember the afternoon they had paired him with a woman about Nadia's size. His task was to overpower the female officer. It made his arm and lower back twinge just thinking about the results of that encounter.

Nadia continued, "I carry my own electroshock protection as well. It scared me, as a teenager, to see my dad as upset as he was. Once I was old enough and could afford it, I bought an electronic control device. I don't have it with me on this trip. I left it back home in Buenos Aires. But I know how it works and I know its potential to stop an attacker."

"Well, I guess I've been informed and warned," Jack said. "I guess, in spite of all that, you have put my mind at ease as far as you being a suspect. I'm truly sorry to hear about what happened to your dad."

"It's changed his life forever. But he's really happy in the new location. I don't worry about him nearly so much anymore."

Chapter Eleven

Jack was concerned with the lack of interest Officer Charles Roast was showing in a case that, even for a hardened cop had so many obvious indications of foul play. He almost seemed bored with having to be involved with the inconvenience of Oscar Dempster. And he seemed to have drawn his conclusions and then closed his mind to anything else.

Officer Roast reminded Jack of another officer he knew very well.

Keegan Willis was a man like that. He would look at a crime scene, or interview a suspect, and immediately conclude that whatever idea materialized in his mind was the last word on the case. It had always been a frustration to Jack, when the two men had worked side by side.

One of Willis's problems was that, though he had been well trained by the folks at the police academy in Aylmer, Ontario, he also took some of his instructions from television. His demeanor changed depending on the characterization he might have seen the night before. Willis was always frustrated, too, that the pathologists couldn't solve crimes as quickly as the actors on the crime scene investigation shows he liked to watch.

I wonder what Keegan would think of this one? Jack thought.

He excused himself and headed up the aisle to talk to Stewart again.

Nadia turned back to alternating between the window and Harry Potter, both of which seemed to be competing for her attention.

Jack's involvement with matters relating to the Dempsters had not escaped the attention of other passengers. As he tried to make his way to where Stewart was standing, a hand would grip Jack's arm or a body would block his progress. The question was always the same. "What's going on? Did that man kill himself?"

The answer, for now, was always the same too. "I can't say."

Truly, Jack couldn't say. He couldn't talk about his suspicions and still continue his makeshift investigation.

I really need Roast to start caring, he thought. *Do I dare to press my case?*

He decided that it was time for a heart-to-heart with

the police officer. He could brace himself for any opposition while hunting down the elusive law man.

"Um, Stewart."

The coach attendant's head snapped up from the paper he was reading.

"Oh, hi, Mr. Elton, er, Jack. What can I do for you?"

"Officer Roast. You seen him around?"

"Not since his whirlwind tour this morning. Give me a sec. I'll check with some of the other guys."

Stewart pulled a walkie-talkie from his belt and called out to the other attendants to ask if they had seen a stranger in a blue suit who looked bored with his lot in life.

"This may take a moment or two, Jack. The other guys and gals may be tied up with other things. I'm assuming you don't want me to make public mention of the events that we've experienced today. These things can be loud," he said, indicating his two-way radio, "and our guests sometimes have exceptional hearing."

It was clear that Stewart was getting into the spirit of the investigation and beginning to enjoy his privileged position in the confidence of the private eye.

"Any idea, just off the top of your head, where I should start looking?" Jack asked.

"I'd put my money on the lounge car or one of the observation domes," Stewart replied. "He likes to flash his badge and strut around, even though he doesn't appear to be doing much. Either place would give him the comfort he appears to crave and, I must admit, the food is a little better and more plentiful. Maybe he's doing a little research for the case."

"I have my doubts," Jack said. "He's already made it known his mind is made up. He's not planning on going any deeper without some severe prodding."

"Coach A-2, are you there?" The attendant's radio crackled. "Stewart, it's Britney in D-5. Your guy's upstairs. Want me to send him to you?"

"D-5 is back there," Stewart said, pointing.

He looked to Jack for an answer to Britney's question.

"Tell her, thanks. I'll go to him, if you'll give me a pass to the higher-priced seats."

Stewart conveyed the message and returned his radio to its holster.

"You go wherever you need to go," he said. "Anyone gives you grief, you have them call me. This thing's always on."

He patted the walkie-talkie.

"Thanks. I appreciate that," Jack said, and headed toward the rear of the train and the wonders of Discovery Class.

It was evident that Stewart had called ahead to Britney to let her know the visitor was on his way. The young woman was waiting in the vestibule of coach D-5 as Jack pushed through the door of the car just ahead of it in the train's consist.

"Hello, sir. I'm Britney. The man you're looking for

is through that door." She pointed behind her. "The stairs are to your right. Watch your head going up. It's a little tight. I take it you know what he looks like. You don't need me up there?"

"No, thanks. By the way, my name is Jack. Nice to meet you, Britney."

The attendant led the way through the door and pointed Jack up the narrow staircase into the dome of the observation coach.

The private eye ascended into the air-conditioned atmosphere of the upper level and advanced down the aisle toward Charles Roast, who was sitting, gazing out at the passing scenery. He was looking at a small spiral notebook as Jack approached. He quickly closed it and stuffed it into an inside pocket when he recognized his visitor.

"Hey, you're not supposed to come up here, are you?"

The police officer sounded surprised, Jack thought. Actually, more than surprised. It was like the reaction one gets from a child who has been caught with his hand in the cookie jar.

"Let's just say, I have friends in lower places, if you catch my drift."

Jack indicated the lower level with an index finger.

Roast gave a weak smile.

"Beautiful view from up here," Jack said. "You like trains?"

"Yeah, I guess. I'm more into flying than this, but I suppose it's good for a change, or if you're not in a hurry."

"Safe to say, you're not in a hurry today, officer?"

"Is that supposed to mean something?" Roast asked, losing every last vestige of his feeble smile.

"Nope. Not a thing. Just making conversation," Jack said.

"You still riding your hobby horse about Mr. Dempster?" the officer asked.

"Let's just say I'm having trouble leaving my work back at home."

"Let me put your mind to rest," Roast offered. "I've checked it out. I'm happy with my conclusions. Soon, it will be in someone else's hands. After that, I'm going back home to my wife, and we're going away on vacation."

"I think I'll just keep on asking questions a little longer," Jack said.

"Suit yourself," Roast replied, and turned toward the window of the domed car.

He turned back quickly to face Jack.

"Look," the officer said, with emphasis, "I'm the guy who got called to mind the body until we get some place where people I'm willing to admit are more knowledgeable than I am can play their game of cut and paste with Mr. Dempster and come to some conclusions. With any luck, I'll be long gone before they have anything to report, assuming there is anything. Let them draw their conclusions. Then someone—not I— can investigate.

"You see," Jack said, frustration evidently rising like

the red hue that was climbing above his shirt collar, "I believe this man had enemies. He wasn't liked by a lot of folks and was losing friends with every passing moment on this train. Maybe he said something that raised someone's hackles. I don't know. Maybe he owed someone money."

Officer Roast gave a sigh of resignation. He nodded slowly.

"Okay," he said. "And here I thought I was in for a nice, easy day and a quick flight home."

Chapter Twelve

The *Last Spike Special* rumbled along the shores of the North Thompson River, on its way to Calgary where, unless it was held for the forensic specialists, it would be turned around overnight and prepared for the trip back to Vancouver.

In the coach where Oscar Dempster had begun his morning and ended his life, it was becoming more difficult to tell that tragedy had struck this little band of travelers. There was no more wringing of hands. Though the conversations were more subdued, the topic of conversation had ceased to be about Oscar Dempster.

Ruby Dempster had calmed down substantially. Val Elton remained with her now, more for company than for comfort. The recent widow was finally managing to keep her makeup presentable without constantly chewing off the lipstick or running her mascara.

Stewart was finally able to return to some semblance of his regular duties. He had announced to his guests that, later in the afternoon, the train would pass through the Spiral Tunnels. These wonders of engineering had been built in 1907 to reduce the grade that trains had to climb to make their way from the town of Field to the Kicking Horse Pass. These tunnels, cut into Mount Ogden and Cathedral Mountain, added distance to the trip for the sake of making it easier to negotiate the route.

From the right vantage point, travelers on the highway in view of the tracks could watch a train of suitable length disappear into the lower tunnel and see the engine emerge higher up the slope before the last car had disappeared into the mountain. The view would be memorable, Stewart said, and everyone was advised to have their cameras ready and to make sure that the batteries were strong and there was sufficient film.

Many of the travelers appeared to take note of the advice. Most appeared to be more excited about the announcement that lunch would soon be served.

Nadia had set down her book and was gazing out at the scenery. She rested her chin in her hand. She had folded her legs under herself. The sun shining in the window illuminated her light-brown skin.

Judge Marshall was standing just inside the door at the rear of the coach. He was attempting to place another call on his cell phone but appeared to be receiving no answer. He cupped a hand to one eye and leaned toward the window leading to the vestibule, as if verifying that there was no one else in the space between the coaches.

When he opened the door, the roar of air and metallic sounds of the couplings filled the rail car. He stepped out onto the little platform, and the door shut behind him.

"Just down this way is where we put him," Jack said.

Officer Charles Roast gave a grunt. He was dragging down the aisle behind the private eye.

The converted sleeper car that the two men were in was used as a sort of office space for the railway employees.

Some of the sleeping cabins had been converted into small lounges with a couple of easy chairs and a small table. The folding beds had been removed.

"I want you to have a look at some marks that you might have missed on your first encounter with Oscar," Jack said, as they approached the location where the subject of their investigation lay.

Oscar Dempster was in one of the few unchanged suites. They had stripped the bed when they brought him in and covered it with plastic sheeting. They had used another of the waterproof covers to wrap the body from head to toe.

Jack tried the door and then remembered that it had

been locked by the trainman. It took him a few moments to track the man down.

When he returned, Jack found Officer Roast leaning against the wall of the corridor, examining his nails, and looking thoroughly disenchanted with his lot in life. He pushed himself fully upright when he saw the two men approaching.

The trainman retrieved the key from his pocket, unlocked the door, and turned the handle. The door opened slightly and a weak smell of death rode out on the blast of cold air that swept into the hallway. He nodded to Jack, then to Roast, pocketed the key again, and returned to his paperwork in the small office where Jack had found him.

"What did you want me to see?" Roast asked. He still sounded impatient.

"I'll show you as soon as I can," Jack said, carefully unwrapping the package that contained the late Oscar Dempster.

Roast made no movement to help with the task but continued to examine his fingers. Apparently finding a hangnail, he nibbled absentmindedly at the offending digit.

Dempster's head and shoulders had finally been freed from the cocoon of the plastic sheet. Jack turned him gently to one side.

"See here?" he asked. "These two spots are the sort of mark that might be left by an electroshock device, something like a small Taser ECD. Oscar was talking about a weak heart yesterday. A mild shock, to him, might have a more dramatic effect than, say, someone of a more stable constitution. Someone immobilized him and then finished him off."

"I'm not convinced," the officer said. "Those marks could be from something else entirely."

"What else could it be?" Jack asked.

"I don't really know," came the reply. "All I know is that Oscar Dempster seemed healthy enough to me. It would take more than a shot from a stun gun to put him away."

"I agree with you there," Jack said.

Roast gave a puzzled look and shrugged his shoulders.

"You finished?" he asked.

"For now," Jack said.

"I'll look into it . . . later," the officer said.

"By then, it may be too late."

Officer Roast walked away.

Once Jack had made sure that Oscar was once more safely wrapped up, he went in search of the trainman. He was easier to find this time, not having completed his paperwork for the morning.

"Maybe I should just give you the key and be done with it."

The man's name was Jerry. He had worked on the railroad all his adult life. His reward was tending the passengers of this luxury liner of the rails, the *Last Spike Special.*

The two men walked back to what was now Oscar's room.

"I'd prefer that you held on to the key for now. And please don't open that door for anyone but me, for the time being. Anyone asks you, let me know right away."

"Yeah, sure. What about the cop?"

"Him too," Jack answered. "He wants in there. I'd like to be with him."

"Whatever you say. Your comfort is my business, as we like to say."

"I'd be really comfortable if there wasn't a body in that room in the first place," Jack said.

The door was secured once again, and Jack headed back to his assigned seat and his wife.

This is a bad start to a life-long relationship if we can't be together, even when we're together, Jack mused.

Judge Marshall was standing in the vestibule again, talking into his cell phone. When he saw the private eye coming, he gave a little wave with his free hand, and then turned away, still speaking into the device. He did not look happy.

Jack entered the coach to discover that Stewart had already begun his lunch rounds. The attendant was past the point in the car where he would have served Jack and Val.

He smiled as Jack entered, reached into his service cart, and brought out a foam box with a clear plastic lid.

"The lady up ahead said you'd prefer beef over the tuna. I saved this one for you. We were running low."

"Thanks," Jack said. "I appreciate all your help."

Stewart gave the investigator a knowing look and moved his cart to one side to let him pass.

Val had almost finished her lunch by the time Jack arrived back in his seat. She was looking out the window.

"You mad?" Jack asked.

Valerie shook her head.

"Just tired," she said. "I had been hoping for so much more. I guess we just have to put things off for a little while."

Now she looked at her husband and smiled. Then she gazed up into his face and kissed him.

"I hope you'll be able to start your vacation by the time we get to the end of this trip," she said.

"You and me both," Jack replied.

As the early afternoon progressed, Jack sat, thinking about the investigation that he had taken on only hours earlier.

It was difficult to comprehend why anyone would commit murder in the middle of a train trip. Questions swirled in his mind.

Was Oscar Dempster killed on the spur of the moment? Was someone so upset with the man's antics that they just snapped and decided to stun the old guy? Who would carry such a device?

Nadia had admitted to owning one, but if she was to

be believed, she had left it at home, on another continent.

Others on board might carry them for protection, but short of examining everyone's baggage, there was no way to know for sure. Jack could probably eliminate anyone who responded to a call for a show of hands.

That would be interesting, he thought, and smiled. *I can just hear the laughter when I say, Hold up your hands if you carry arms.*

After immobilizing Oscar, if it were a spontaneous thing, did the murderer strangle him in a rage? Was he subdued just so he could be strangled?

He'd have had to make you awfully mad to make you lash out at him like that, Jack thought.

There was, of course, the possibility that someone on the train had planned this for some time. Could an individual learn of someone's travel plans and then make reservations on the same conveyance in order to have the opportunity to seek revenge?

It didn't seem likely. There were, though, hundreds of travelers on this train. Any one of them could be a killer.

But then, the *Last Spike Special* ran under rigid restrictions. Passengers were not permitted to travel between coaches during most of the journey. During the early morning, when Oscar had met his end, the coach in which Jack was presently traveling had been, like all the others, reserved for only those who had seat assignments in that car.

Jack had noticed, early on, how efficient the coach attendants were at keeping their guests together. Except for railway crew members and Officer Roast, no stranger had entered the coach all day.

Jack felt confident he could limit his suspects to those who now were settling back in their seats, well fed and relaxed. Some were, no doubt, looking forward to the end of the day and a comfortable hotel bed.

After two days on the swaying coach, many would be surprised to discover, after leaving the train, that they still experienced a phantom feeling of movement once they were on solid ground.

Will I find the answers in time? Jack wondered.

His answer came in the form of an announcement from Stewart.

Since the conclusion of the meal service, the train had slowed to almost a crawl. This was not unusual, given the nature of the trip. When passing points of interest, the train would be slowed to allow everyone the opportunity to gawk out the windows at some wonder of nature. Those who were quick enough would run to the vestibule to get an unobstructed view, free from the window reflections that could ruin a good photo.

From time to time it was wildlife by the side of the tracks that drew people's attention. On those occasions, the train slowed for the safety of passengers and the animals, as well as for the view. A moose or a bear on the tracks was a definite hazard. Encounters with either had been known to damage the engine and on occasion derail cars.

Fortunately for the *Last Spike Special*, there had never been an accident of that sort.

Now, though, it appeared that the train had been moving unusually slow for a long time. There was nothing outside the windows but the view of the river valley. Occasionally, they would pass over a bridge to the other side. This process would be repeated numerous times before their journey came to an end.

"Ladies and gentlemen," Stewart began, "we are going to be delayed on our journey. We will not arrive in Calgary until much later this evening."

An assortment of groans and voiced complaints filled the air.

Stewart continued, "There has been an accident a little farther up the line. Some freight cars jumped the rails and the train is blocking the line. It's on a section of the route that is double tracked, and we had hoped that we could sneak around the trouble, but the repair crew has arrived with their crane to put the cars back on the rails. To do their job, they need to use that section of track we had been hoping to get to first. Since we don't have the right of way, we will have to wait and enjoy this beautiful mountain scenery."

More groaning and complaining ensued.

"Please do not leave the coach. I must warn you, especially, not to get off the train. I know it's tempting and in a moment we will be standing still, but we could start moving at any moment. Calgary is still a long way away. It would be a very tiring walk. And dangerous too."

Jack looked around.

Some folks had snatched pillows from their over-head racks and were busy preparing for an afternoon siesta. As long as they weren't moving, they could close their eyes for awhile and not miss anything.

Others buried their noses in books and newspapers.

There was an evident spirit of resignation among most of the passengers.

Jack knew a good thing when he saw it. A least it was good for his investigation.

Folks were willing to talk more freely when they weren't distracted by other things. Now that they were sitting on the edge of a river valley there were some, he was convinced, who might appreciate the opportunity to strike up a conversation.

He looked around for his first candidates. He settled on an older couple sitting toward the rear of the coach, close to where the cross of duct tape marked the door to the scene of the crime.

The De Jongs were visiting from the Netherlands. They had just arrived in Canada a couple of days be-fore the train trip was scheduled to begin. Their daugh-ter and son-in-law lived south of Edmonton, in Leduc, where the discovery of oil had marked the beginning of the Alberta oil boom many years earlier.

They made Jack's job a little easier, from the start.

"Wasn't that too bad about that man this morning," Mrs. De Jong said, after Jack had introduced himself. "Imagine coming on a nice trip only to commit suicide. It's tragic."

"What did you see this morning? Was there anything unusual?" Jack asked.

The couple looked surprised at the question.

"You're not suggesting anything criminal, are you?" Jake De Jong asked.

"Oh, no," Jack lied. "I was just wondering about Mr. Dempster's appearance. Did you see him at all before he went into the washroom?"

"Not really," Jake said. "He walked past me. I was sitting right here, on the aisle. He looked just like he did yesterday. Maybe not quite so angry, though."

"He scared me a little bit yesterday," Mrs. De Jong said. "And I'm used to people who complain a lot."

She looked at her husband as she spoke and smiled. Apparently Jake De Jong had had his share of flare-ups.

"This will sound strange, I know," Jack said, "but did you notice anything else—anything unusual—going on at this end of the coach?"

"I can't say that I did," Jake said.

"Not me, either," his wife added.

"People were traveling back and forth in the coach," Jake said. "I didn't notice anyone new. I wasn't really paying much attention to what was going on behind me. I heard someone talking, but didn't hear who they were talking to. I didn't want to turn around and seem rude. We missed the continental breakfast at the motel. I wanted my coffee and something to eat."

"That's fine," Jack said, and added, "I'm just trying to help Mrs. Dempster sort out some questions about what happened to her husband today. You never know what might be helpful."

"That poor dear," Mrs. De Jong said, shaking her head sadly.

All three agreed that Ruby Dempster was facing a challenging future.

After exchanging a few pleasantries and their concerns about the slow progress of their trip, Jack excused himself. He promised to return later. The De Jongs were anxious to talk about their home country.

"I'd like to bring my wife to meet you when I come. She'd love to hear about Holland. She'd like to visit there some day. Me too."

As he began his slow trip down the coach, Jack felt a tug at his sleeve. He turned to see a serious-looking young man in a T-shirt and jeans. His partner was a pleasant-looking woman with long, dark, curly hair. She wore a cotton floral-print dress that went to her ankles and sandals.

"I see you are asking questions about this morning," the man said. "I'd like to talk to you."

"Sure," Jack said, sitting on the arm of the seat across the aisle from the couple.

The seat's occupant had obviously decided to go elsewhere in the coach during the delay.

Various passengers had begun to form small groups throughout the car. With Stewart's help, some of the seats had been turned around so that they faced each other.

At least they are getting to know one another a little better, Jack thought. *The delay isn't a total waste of time.*

He turned his attention to the young man, who was now hanging over the aisle, toward him. He was anxious to speak to Jack.

"Listen," the man said. "I've been watching what's been going on today. I think that man was murdered."

"Shhh . . ." Jack said, holding an index finger to his lips. "You'll frighten people with a statement like that. Why do you make such an outrageous claim?"

The man looked up and down the coach a couple of times before continuing, "I think it was aliens. That's what I think."

"You mean folks from another country?" Jack asked.

"Another planet" came the emphatic reply.

It takes all kinds of people, Jack thought.

"What makes you think that?" he asked.

"Voices. I heard voices. Kind of off-in-the-distance voices. I think they were going to abduct that man. And when he resisted, you know what I think happened? Do ya?"

"I can't imagine," Jack said.

"I think they got inside his head and made him do that to himself."

"That's certainly a unique possibility," Jack said. "And you, ma'am. Did you hear anything?"

The woman smiled.

"I was abducted once," she said. "Nope. Didn't hear anything. But then, Greg here, he's more tuned into that stuff than I am. We're the Guthries, by the way. I'm Hannah."

She stuck out her hand. It was cold and a little too moist for Jack's liking.

"Listen folks," he said, "I'll keep your thoughts in mind. I'm just getting some information together so I can give a little comfort to Mrs. Dempster. It might be best if I break that kind of news to her. Thanks for your help."

Jack wasn't convinced that there was anything of value in what the Guthries had had to share, but he filed everything at the back of his mind.

Just in case, he thought.

The screeching of metal and the lurching of the train brought everyone to full attention.

Jack was almost thrown to the floor by the sudden movement.

Chapter Thirteen

"Nothing to worry about, folks," Stewart said, into his microphone. "We just need to move out of the way a little. There is a repair crew coming up behind us, and they can't get by until we back up to the last siding. It will be a little slow, and you're going to see where you've been, but hopefully, with a few more hands on the scene up ahead, we'll be able to get moving a little more quickly. Hang tight. I'll put on the kettle for tea."

Some folks smiled. Some applause could be heard on the announcement of snacks to be served. Most continued what they had been doing before the interruption.

I may have to step up the pace a little, Jack thought.

The sudden lurching of the train that led to Stewart's announcement had resulted in the private eye throwing himself into the first empty seat he could find. He discovered that he was sitting beside the young medical student again.

"Welcome back, my friend."

Her voice was tinted with the coloration of her native Spanish language.

"We've got to stop meeting like this." Jack smiled.

"I'm afraid we will be inseparable for a few more hours," Nadia said, flashing perfect white teeth.

"Any more thoughts on this whole situation?" Jack asked.

"I heard your conversation with that young couple, the Guthries. They seem to have an interesting perspective on things. Not scientifically based, I think, but intriguing nevertheless."

Jack lowered his voice.

"There are folks like that all over the world. I think some are seriously misled. Others are engaging in wishful thinking. Others might benefit from a session with the folks in your profession and some prescription drugs."

"Take it easy, my friend," the doctor-to-be replied, to Jack's obvious dismay.

"What?" he asked.

"I'll admit that most of what they said is a little far out. But I have learned that folks with strong beliefs like that incorporate reality into what they think and their interpretation of circumstances.

"I didn't hear the whole conversation, but I think you should analyze what they said. Don't hesitate to go back to them for clarification. You may discover some little gem of truth that will help you to conclude your investigation.

"Want me to help? I'm almost finished my book. It looks like I'll have some time on my hands. I'm going to wait until I'm in my nice cozy hotel room before I read the end of the story. It will put a nice end on my very eventful day."

"Maybe a little later," Jack said. "I've got a few more people I need to talk to before *my* eventful day is done."

"*Hasta luego,* my friend. See you later," she said, as Jack slipped out of the seat.

Jack decided to stop by his own seat and see how Val was doing. It was obvious, by now, that he would need some plans for the future to make up for this turn of events that had made their honeymoon into another crime investigation. It seemed, to Jack, that no matter how fast he tried to run, trouble always seemed to catch up with him.

"How's Mrs. Elton doing?" he asked, as he sat down heavily.

"I don't feel much like Mrs. Elton today," she replied. "I've hardly seen you all day. I mean you've been in view, but you've spent most of your time with the other passengers and that strange police officer, Roast. I hope you're not getting too attached to the cute *chica* sitting near the back."

Val smiled, but Jack could tell that his consultations

with the young medical student were causing her some concern.

"Honey, she's giving me some advice from a medical standpoint. I've just come from having an interesting talk about the possibility of alien involvement in Mr. Dempster's murder."

"People from another country?" Valerie asked, looking serious.

"We really do think alike. That was my reaction too. No. A couple toward the back are sailing the theory that creatures from elsewhere might have been responsible."

"I'm sorry, Jack. I'm too tired for that sort of thing right now. You deal with that one on your own. I'm not really in a reasonable mood this afternoon, and a suggestion like that will either get me angry or giggling so badly that I'll be no further use to anyone."

"How's Ruby making out?" Jack asked.

"Coming along, I think. I've been able to leave her alone for most of the afternoon. Poor dear dropped off to sleep a little while ago."

Val turned peered through the space between the backs of the seats before continuing.

"She still appears dead to the world back there. Sorry. Bad choice of words, I guess. She's resting. I think that will help. She's going to need her strength once this thing gets out. What's with that police officer? Is he any help at all?"

"He is being rather hard to convince at the moment. He seems so tied up in the fact that his vacation is coming up that he wants to avoid a lot of involvement with the present case."

"That is strange," Val said. "It seems, though, that I heard something about dereliction of duty, if I remember my police training. I'm pretty certain that he has an obligation to pursue any reasonable leads and to take seriously any information passed on in good faith. I wouldn't push the alien aspect too hard, though."

"I hadn't thought of that—the dereliction of duty thing," Jack said. "Maybe it comes from being away from the force for a while. Maybe I need to take another tack with this guy. Maybe I need to press a little harder."

"That's the way, Jack. I know you can't sit still when there's a good crime brewing. Don't worry about me. I'm happy when you're happy. This stuff makes you happy, doesn't it?"

Jack smiled.

"I promise I'll make it up to you, as soon as I can," he said. "You start thinking about where you'd like to go. I'll try to make it happen."

He stood to leave.

"One more thing, Jack," Valerie said. "Don't let him intimidate you. Remember, witnesses cannot be prosecuted for their testimony. You tell him what you think and why, and if he can prove you wrong, so be it. But he can't get you punished for what you believe to be true."

"Thanks," Jack said, and went in search of the elusive Charles Roast.

* * *

As Jack headed out of the coach once again, he was thinking about what Nadia had said about there being some kernel of truth in the testimony of the Guthries.

I wonder what I can believe, he thought.

He entered the dome car once more and ascended the stairs. The attendant was not in sight. He hoped he wasn't going to get a severe talking to for not obtaining the proper permission before entering the domain of those able to afford a more luxurious trip.

Roast is taking liberties with his position of author-ity, he thought. *Pulling rank and then just slacking off. I wonder what ethics course he took.*

As before, the officer was sitting near the front of the dome car. He had a cell phone to his ear and was concluding his conversation as Jack drew alongside.

"Back again, I see. Got anything new? Or just the same old stuff? I thought you were on vacation."

"I was, actually. But there has been a crime committed, and I can't seem to get any police back-up."

"The way I see it, I have no further obligations," Roast replied. "Believe me, I am doing my job. I am protecting the innocent and administering justice. You just can't see it."

As he replaced his cell phone in a leather holster on his belt, Jack took note of the fact that the officer had boarded the train prepared for every eventuality short of a riot. His department apparently believed that its officers should be fully equipped.

The only thing missing was the billy club that would ordinarily have been suspended by the metal ring on the right side of Roast's service belt. Jack did not ask whether the gun was loaded. He took a mental inventory.

"Well?" Roast asked.

Jack had been immersed in thought.

"Huh? What was that?" he asked. "Oh, yeah. What I was going to say was that I believe there has been a crime committed. I have every reason to believe that the perpetrator is still onboard. And, I think that if we do not act quickly, a murderer may get away."

"I'll be happy to listen to your theory and any evidence you think you might have," Roast said. "No promises. You talk. I'll listen. Don't think I'm not paying attention if I look at the scenery while you share your morsels of wisdom."

"Great," Jack said.

"You're welcome."

Might as well go for it, Jack thought, and launched into his talk about what he knew and suspected.

"We've got this guy and his wife who get on the train yesterday along with the rest of us. Well, not exactly with us, but close enough. He's obnoxious, but no worse than some, from what I hear from the coach attendant. Maybe someone wasn't as tolerant.

"This morning he visits the washroom. While he's cleaning up, someone comes in, stuns him, and then strangles the life out of him."

"So tell me," Roast asked, not bothering to take his eyes off the passing scenery, "How does this 'person unknown' get into the washroom with Dempster? Don't you think he would lock the door?"

"I know I would," Jack said. "But, suppose he was just combing his hair or washing his face. I sometimes leave the lock off, in case someone needs to get in."

"Maybe," Roast said.

"Could be he knew whoever it was and opened the door," Jack added.

"That would certainly limit your suspects. Who did he know?" Roast asked.

"Far as I can tell, his wife, Ruby."

"You think she killed her husband? Heaven knows she had good reason, but look at the woman. Do you think she had the strength to strangle her husband to death? I think your theory just went bust."

"I wonder if there was someone else on board who knew him," Jack asked.

Roast continued to scan the countryside.

"Well, you could ask, but I'll bet ya that no one is going to confess to that, for fear of being found out. Do any of them know about your theory?"

Jack suddenly decided that it would be best to keep some things to himself.

"I think I'd better have a talk with Ruby Dempster," he said.

"Knock yourself out," Roast said, and returned to his sightseeing.

Jack stood and walked to the end of the coach. As he turned to descend the stairs to the lower level, he noticed that the officer was on his cell phone again.

Jack made his way back through the vestibule and into the coach where he was convinced the killer of Oscar Dempster would be found.

Ruby Dempster had awakened from her sleep.

"Do you mind if I ask you a few more questions?"

Jack sat down beside the sad-looking woman.

"No. Go ahead," she said. "I have some questions of my own that I don't suppose anyone is going to be able to answer."

"I was wondering—Is there anyone else on the train that you know? Is there anyone who might be able to help you, once we arrive at Calgary?"

Jack was not about to reveal his true motive. As far as he knew, Ruby Dempster had every reason to believe that her husband had taken his own life.

His real reason for asking was to find out if there was anyone Ruby could identify who might have a motive for killing her husband.

"There is no one that we knew before we got on the train yesterday," she answered. "At least, as far as I know. Oscar didn't mention knowing anyone on board, before he . . . before he . . ."

The woman dissolved in tears.

Jack had an answer to his question. He wondered if it was borne out by the facts. Surely someone knew Oscar

Dempster. It was that individual who had taken the man's life.

But, why? Jack wondered.

"You're a great help."

The private investigator immediately recognized Val's voice.

"I'm sorry. I didn't mean to make Mrs. Dempster cry. I just asked an innocent question."

"Let me in there. I'll sit with Ruby until she calms down again," Valerie said quietly.

Jack excused himself and stood up. His wife slid into the seat he had just vacated. She took out a tissue and gave it to the grieving woman.

Judge Marshall had returned from his latest trip out to the vestibule. He was sitting with Toulouse Gravelle. The two men were talking quietly together. Jack decided to join them.

"Good afternoon, gentlemen. How is your trip going?" he asked.

The judge opened his mouth to speak, but before he could utter a word, Gravelle jumped in.

"Perfectly lousy, if you ask me," he said. "I came on this trip for a nice relaxing time. I had been looking forward to an uneventful voyage, but look at what I got. There's a dead man riding with us.

"Now, I'll freely admit that I didn't like him at all. In other circumstances, I might have helped him do what he did back there this morning."

He nodded toward the door with the duct tape across it.

"I'd be really careful about a confession like that, sonny," the judge piped in. "If a fella was looking for suspects in a murder, he might just take that as evidence that you might be hiding something."

Gravelle's face went beet red.

"Oh, no, Monsieur Judge Marshall. I could never do a thing like that. That is wrong, I tell you. That is not the way we should settle differences. I only meant that the man was annoying. He was rude to people who wanted to help him, or just wanted to be his friend. Oh, no. I would never, ever consider killing a man. Anyway, it doesn't matter, in this case. It is obvious that he sui-cided. Um, how do you English people say it? He com-mitted suicide. That's it. He took his own life."

"I'm not sure that you could convince Mr. Elton about that," Judge Marshall said, and gave a brief sample of his unusual laugh. "I believe that Jack, here, has another theory. Do you want to tell him, or shall I?" he asked.

"I'm sure I don't know what you mean, sir," Jack said, knowing exactly what the judge was inferring.

"I think you know precisely what I mean. I've been watching and listening. You seem to think that this thing is a . . ." He lowered his voice as he spoke the fi-nal word, "murder."

"You don't really, do you?" Gravelle asked with gen-uine surprise.

"Well, I . . ." Jack began.

"Of course he does," the judge said. "He thinks he's got evidence that someone crept up on the old fella and 'done him in,' as Eliza Doolittle would say."

"Doolittle?" Gravelle asked. "I've not heard of a Doolittle in the coach."

Judge Marshall sounded like he was about to swallow his tongue. He began to shake with laughter.

"You poor, illiterate man. Eliza Doolittle is the female character in *My Fair Lady*. She is definitely *not* on the train. It's just a phrase she used in a conversation she was having with . . . oh, never mind. Mr. Elton believes that someone killed Mr. Dempster earlier today. Got that?"

Gravelle nodded.

"I don't believe it," the politician said.

"Ask him," the judge said.

"Let's just say that you're correct, Judge Marshall," Jack said. "I'd really like to know where you get your information. Was it something I said?"

"For now, let's just say I have my way of finding things out. And you've been talking to a lot of folks since this morning. That certainly raises some suspicion about your motives."

"What if I told you that I just wanted to get to know my fellow passengers a little better?" Jack asked.

"I'd throw the book at you for perjury," the judge replied.

"You seem rather confident," Jack said.

"You may not appear to convince some others, but

you have my attention, Jack. I'm going to keep an eye on you."

Judge William Marshall smiled and leaned his head back on the headrest of his seat. He closed his eyes.

"Carry on with your investigation, officer," he said, and gave a dismissive gesture with his hand.

Jack rose to leave. He headed toward Stewart's station. From behind him, he heard the voice of Toulouse Gravelle.

"Is that true? Do you really believe that it was—"

Jack cut him off, before he had a chance to say something that would cause irreversible and, he felt, premature concern among the other passengers.

"Sit down," Jack whispered, with urgency in his voice. "I believe that the death of Mr. Dempster was not all that it at first appeared. I'm trying to get all the facts straight before I jump to any conclusions. It would be an immense help to me, sir, if you would keep this information to yourself. As a politician, surely you know how a misplaced word can cause no end of trouble. I'm relying on you to handle this with great discretion."

Gravelle nodded his agreement.

"That is *tragique*," he said, once again mixing French and English, a common trait of those used to speaking in two different languages on a regular basis.

"Let me do what I must," Jack said. "I'll let you know if I come up with anything."

"*D'accord*. I agree," came the reply.

Jack resumed his mission to speak with Stewart.

Chapter Fourteen

The private investigator found Stewart in his little storage space at the end of the coach. It seemed to Jack that the coach attendant spent a lot of his time preparing to serve yet more food to a coach full of passengers with a growing need—not for more calories, but of more exercise.

Stewart looked up from a case of soft drinks that he was sorting and loading into his metal cart.

"Mr. Elton . . . I mean, Jack. What's on your mind? Can I offer some assistance to you?"

"I was just thinking," Jack said. "If this had happened— the murder, I mean—on solid ground, I might have had a few more resources at my command. As it is, I'm stuck with just what I can round up onboard.

"You're an immense help, but you have a job to tend

to. I have some medical expertise in the young woman by the window. She's a medical student. I'd like to say that I have some police support, but I'm getting a little stressed out by Officer Roast's unwillingness, or inability, to act. Either he doesn't believe me, or he chooses to let someone else do the investigation. His major concern seems to be his own comfort. I'd actually like to check his credentials. But, how do we do that out here in the valley. If I could get close to a computer and hook up to the Internet, I could . . ."

Stewart's head snapped up, and he looked at Jack with a grin on his face.

"I think I might have a solution to your problem. This isn't the Wild West anymore, you know. Look at all those empty telephone poles going by. Look at the situation we are in, sitting on a siding waiting for a train to pass. How do you think we knew they wanted us to move when we have no visible means of communication?"

The attendant stood up, set down his cardboard case, and headed down the aisle.

"Follow me, please," he called over his shoulder.

Jack walked behind like an obedient puppy.

What sort of surprise am I going to experience now? he wondered.

Stewart entered the next coach where Oscar Dempster was traveling in air-conditioned luxury. It was here, too, where railway staff did their paperwork and caught a few moments rest, before returning to their public duties, visible to the passengers.

He stopped before an open door and, with a sweeping motion of his hand, indicated that Jack should enter.

"I think you might find some assistance in here," he said.

"You know, I think I just might," Jack replied, turning to shake Stewart's hand.

"I'll leave you to it."

He indicated an older man sitting at a desk.

"This is Dave Cooke. He'll be able to answer any questions you have. I'll get back to my other guests."

"Thanks," Jack said, and stuck out his hand to Dave Cooke, who gripped it so tightly that the private investigator winced.

"What do you need?" the man asked.

Stewart had led Jack to the communications center of the *Last Spike Special.*

Though it was limited in size by the necessity of locating it in one of the converted sleeping compartments, it had sufficient provision of electronic gear to allow the train crew to deal with most of the requirements for effective communication.

The progress of the train was tracked by a GPS system. A monitor indicated the exact location of the *Last Spike Special.* This same information was available to the railway dispatchers along the line, who were responsible for ensuring the smooth movement of both passenger and freight trains on their block, in the system of rails and switches under their care. A signal from the train was bounced off a satellite in synchronous orbit above North America and, through electronic wizardry that Jack did not fully understand, was able to track the movement of the coaches to within yards of their location.

A radio communication system ensured that the crew could be in constant voice contact, not only within the coaches, but also with other trains, with the company office, and with emergency services, should the need arise.

What attracted Jack's attention, though, was the computer in front of which Dave Cooke was sitting.

When the man had asked what it was that Jack needed, it was to the computer that the investigator had pointed.

"I never would have thought that this sort of thing was possible," Jack said, as he tapped the keyboard in front of which he was now seated.

"We use a cellular AirLink modem," Cooke replied.

Seeing the quizzical look on Jack's face, he continued. "We are using the cellular service to connect to the Internet. As long as we are in range of a communications cell, we can use the system. As you know, wireless communication has experienced an explosive increase lately. There is hardly a spot where we travel that doesn't receive a good signal. Around the major centers, of course, almost everybody uses a cell phone.

"A lot of folks have completely abandoned their hard-wired phones for wireless ones. A guy in business can be doing his grocery shopping and close a deal or arrange an appointment, by using the cell system exclusively. And he almost never misses an important call. Of course, it can be a bit inconvenient when you're on a family outing. And you can't afford to be using your phone in the theatre. For our purposes, and yours too, I gather, the system can't be beat."

"It may just be the thing that turns this day around," Jack replied.

It was Dave's turn to look confused.

Jack said nothing but pressed on with his search.

The train was still sitting on its siding when Jack reentered the coach and slid into the seat beside Val.

The slow progress of the *Last Spike Special*, and the stress of the day, had obviously taken a toll on Valerie. She sat, feet pulled up underneath her, with her head resting against the window. Her eyes were shut, and she began to rouse from her slumber only after Jack had shaken her gently awake.

"Oh, hi. I must have drifted off for a moment. What's new?"

"You'd be proud of their communications center, Val. I think we're safe."

"That's nice," Valerie replied, and looked as though she might be preparing to settle back into sleep.

"I made some interesting discoveries," Jack said. "I've got a theory that I need to try to prove before we get into Calgary."

"That's nice," Valerie said again, snuggling up to the back of her seat.

"What do you think of Charles Roast?" he asked.

"I try not to think about him at all" came the groggy reply. "I haven't had much contact with the man. You're the one with the face-to-face experience. I gather you have an opinion."

"I do," Jack said. "I'm trying to figure the man out. He doesn't fit my concept of what a police officer should be. He doesn't seem anxious to investigate any more than necessary. It's almost as if he doesn't enjoy his job."

"Or, maybe, just not *this* job."

"What does that mean?" Jack asked.

"Maybe he's trying to hide something. Maybe solving this case is not in his best interests. I don't know. I'm supposed to be on vacation—my honeymoon, actually. I think, maybe, you should be too."

"That's an interesting thought," Jack said.

"What? That you should be on vacation?"

"No. Not that. I'll see ya later. Enjoy your rest."

"Whatever," Val replied groggily and snuggled deeper on to the back of her seat. Her eyes closed.

Jack wasn't sure whether he had been dismissed by his wife or whether it was just the fatigue of the day's events that had made the conversation draw to such a quick conclusion.

He knew now, though, that he had to move quickly in order to either prove his theory or to conclude that the problem was too big for him to solve. For Jack, the latter conclusion had never been satisfactory.

On the other hand, he wondered just how much longer he could ignore Valerie in the name of justice. Their marriage was certainly off to a strange start.

He had to talk to Officer Roast one more time.

Maybe a nice neighborly chat would be the way to go this time, he thought as he headed back to the observation dome.

As he reached the top of the stairs, he could see that the officer was busy on his cell phone again. The man sat with his legs crossed and toyed with the lace of his left shoe as he spoke, in hushed tones, to whoever his confidante was.

Except for a young couple, barely out of their teens, sitting near the middle of the coach, the police officer had no other company.

With the train still sitting on the siding awaiting the track repairs and the clearing of the line, there was nothing new to see. Most of the passengers had gone to the dining room for a mid-afternoon snack or had returned to their first-class seats to prepare for what, Jack assumed, they hoped would be a quick entry into the city, once this inconvenience was over.

Roast looked over his shoulder and scanned the length of the dome. Seeing Jack, he gave a slight nod and turned back to his exchange.

He had finished his conversation and holstered his phone by the time Jack pulled alongside.

With a hand gesture, Jack waved the man over toward the place by the window to his left. The private investigator took the newly vacated aisle seat.

"Let's call a truce. Since we're going to be in this thing for a while longer, I thought we might take a little time to get to know each other better. Tell me about yourself," Jack said.

"I'm not really in the mood for the bonding thing right now. I've got better things to do," Roast replied.

"Ah, come on," Jack said, sounding jovial. "Where ya going to go? What can you possibly do, sitting out here in the midst of what even the auto club would classify as wilderness, beautiful though it is?"

"Guys like you are the reason I don't go on these kinds of trips. There's always some guy, a salesman or motivational speaker, who wants to glad-hand you and make you feel all warm and fuzzy. It's always 'How does that make you feel' and 'tell me about your journey to this point.' Stuff like that. Or, you get on a plane, hoping to catch some shut-eye before an important presentation, and they put someone beside you with nothing better to do than talk and ask questions. It's not for me."

"And, how does that make you feel?" Jack asked, with a broad grin. "Tell me about how you got to this point in your life."

Roast smiled sincerely, for the first time during his entire time in Jack's presence during the trip.

"Okay. You've got me. I give up. Let's get to the bonding."

"It's not like that," Jack said. "Where ya from?"

"I'm from back east. Southwestern Ontario," Roast replied. "Grew up north of London. Maybe that's why I like it where I am now. It's quieter outside the city. Things move at a more leisurely pace."

"Is that why you're so laid back about our friend Oscar?" Jack asked.

"Well, he's no friend of mine," Roast said. "I can't say I knew too much about him. All I know is that if it weren't for him, I wouldn't be here."

Jack pressed on.

"How about family? You married?"

"Yeah. Heather—my wife—she grew up back east too. We met at the police college in Aylmer. Mind you, she had more motivation to go into police work."

"She an officer too?" Jack asked.

"Yeah. We work together. It's not a particularly big police force. Just four of us, to be honest. Heather's the only female. The other two guys are the chief and a young guy who mostly deals with the bylaw stuff."

"So you get all the big cases," Jack said with a smile.

"Yeah, right," Roast replied. "We get guys breaking into the corner store for a can of pop. Occasionally there will be a dustup in the bar. Those are about as big as they get."

"So how do you end up on this train, dealing with the likes of Oscar Dempster?" Jack asked.

"I was called."

Charles Roast fell suddenly silent.

"Was that your wife I saw in the pickup that delivered you to the station this morning?"

"Yep. That's my girl," Roast replied. "We share a vehicle. Not a big budget for such a small town. We do what we can.

"She grew up with a lawyer for a father. He's a driven man. I gather he was quite a scrapper in his day. Loved his work. It took him places. He passed on his love for justice to his daughter. It seemed like a natural thing for Heather to get involved in some form of legal work."

"But why police?" Jack asked. "Why didn't she follow in her father's footsteps and become a lawyer?"

"Heather's had some serious issues in her life. I'd rather not go into it right now. And then stuff happened that sort of galvanized her resolve to take a more active role in the justice system. It's a long story."

Roast turned his face to the window and fell silent again.

At that moment, there was the loud screeching of the brake shoes of the coach. Ahead, Jack could see the black exhaust of the lead engine as it began its forward movement. He watched in fascination while, one by one, the coaches lurched forward as the tension was taken up on the row of cars. The train was moving again. It was slow, but it was moving.

Gotta pick up the pace, Jack thought. *Time to move on.*

"This has been fascinating, but I should get back to my wife. It's supposed to be my vacation too," he said to the officer moping by the window. "We'll have to do this again sometime."

"Not too soon, I hope," Roast said without turning his head.

Jack headed for the stairs to the lower level.

Now that the train was moving again, Jack had to brace himself against the swaying of the cars. Though its forward progress was slow, the train had to traverse land that was, at times, uneven and, given its rocky composition, not easily made level.

He was surprised at how quickly, it seemed, the caravan of coaches came back to life. No sooner had it begun to move again than passengers began heading, once more, for the dome car, the observation platform at the tail end, and the vestibules between the coaches. Fatigued or not, these folks were still anxious to absorb as much scenery as was available.

Seeing that even Val had roused from her nap, Jack went back to his seat beside her. He needed her to know that he wasn't trying to avoid her. He needed to apologize, he felt, for abandoning her for the thrill of this present chase. He needed to debrief to the officer of the law who had arrested his attention not many months before. Surely she would understand his desire to solve the death of Oscar Dempster.

"Listen, Jack. I knew when I married you that I would have to share you with your obsession, your work, your hobby, that thing that drives you from day to day. I fell in love with you while you were solving a murder. If it hadn't been for the Fukushima case, we probably would never have started seeing one another on a regular basis.

"I'll admit that I felt somewhat abandoned when you were working on the Herties kidnapping, but that was what really confirmed that it was true love. I could hardly bear to be apart. And that's why I married you. At least here, when you leave me, I know you can't be more than a trainlength away. And I'll let you in on a little secret. I still miss you when you're gone, and I'm still madly in love with you when you get back.

"Have fun. Solve your crime. We'll celebrate when you're done. I'm already plotting a pay-back vacation to make up for the separation I've had to endure on my honeymoon."

Valerie Elton threw herself back in her seat, feigning distress, and placed her hand on her forehead like the starlets of the early years of cinema.

"I'm happy to hear you say that," Jack said. "This wasn't in my plans at all, but I've got to do something about Oscar. Somebody has to take responsibility."

"I'll help any way I can, Jack, but for awhile Ruby was my main concern," Valerie said. "I'm never far away, if you need advice."

"I know. And I'm glad," he said.

They both fell silent.

Valerie turned and looked at Jack. She watched him sitting rigidly in his seat. She saw how he was not noticing the passing panorama outside the window.

"Jack, you have my permission to go. I love you. You are free to continue your quest for truth, justice, and the North American way. You're not enjoying just sitting. I can almost hear the wheels grinding in your brain. Be happy. Solve a crime. Go on. I'll wait right here for you."

Jack smiled. He turned to Val and gave her a hug and a kiss on the end of her nose.

"Thanks, hon. I promise I'll make this up to you."

"You can bet on that," Val replied with a grin. "Now get out of my sight you . . . you . . . you husband, you."

Jack didn't need any further encouragement. He was heading down the aisle with determination. He was on a quest for something elusive but he could tell that he was drawing closer.

A few more questions, some good fortune, and a few more answers, and Oscar Dempster might receive some overdue justice, he thought, but he couldn't quite drive away the phrase from a favorite game that kept running through his head. *"Someone, in the washroom, with the rope."*

Chapter Fifteen

"Hey, Mister. What's going on?"

The voice belonged to a short, balding man in brown shorts and a new *Last Spike Special* T-shirt.

"What do you mean?" Jack asked.

Looking down at his inquisitor, he could see his own face reflected back in the silvered lenses of the man's sunglasses.

"I mean, what's going on? You can't fool me. There's something strange going on. I mean, apart from that guy ending up dead."

"How do you mean *strange*," the private investigator asked.

"I've been watching you. You've been talking to people, and from what I have been able to gather, there seems to be more to this than meets the eye."

135

"Well, sir, I'm just trying to make sure that we have as many facts as we can get to share with the police when we arrive at the station later today."

"What about the other guy? He sure looked like a cop to me. Shouldn't he be the one doing the investigating? You're one of the passengers. You a cop too?"

Jack wondered whether the man's red face was the result of his present emotional state, or simply the natural consequence of staring out from the vestibule of the train as it made its slow progress along the valley.

"Yeah, something like that," Jack replied, smiling down at the man. "I'm an officer with the Vancouver Police Department."

"So, what are you getting paid for this? You working with the other guy?" the man asked.

"To be frank, it's not really any of your business but I'm not getting paid for doing this. I'm actually on my honeymoon. Like you said, I'm just a passenger, or at least trying to be. Name's Jack, by the way."

The man removed his sunglasses and stuck out his right hand.

"Myron Foote," he said. "I'm an accountant from New York. Pleased to meet you. So, really, what's going on?"

"I'm really sorry to tell you that not much is going on. The police officer you have seen is just acting as an escort of sorts. I'm not at all sure what he is doing, but I'm sure you'll understand that when someone dies the

way Mr. Dempster did, there are procedures that have to be followed."

Jack was not at all sure what procedures Officer Roast would admit to. He was as much in the dark about the man's purpose as Myron Foote was.

"Dempster? That was his name?" the little man asked. "I saw and heard him yesterday. He was a rather irritating fellow. I wouldn't be surprised to hear that someone killed him. Of course, maybe he just came to the realization that he was a poor specimen of humanity and just did himself in. Sorry, but I don't really have a lot of sympathy for the likes of guys like that," Foote added.

Jack held his tongue.

No use getting into a fruitless debate with this guy about how every death affects others, and how there are some, his widow among them, who loved Oscar Dempster and are also impacted by his death he thought.

"Now if you don't mind," Jack said, "I'm going to go and sit with my wife. We haven't had a lot of quality time together on this trip so far. Trust me, though. Everything is going to be just fine. Enjoy the rest of your trip."

"Yeah, well . . ." Myron said, and put on his sunglasses.

He headed down the aisle muttering to himself.

Jack smiled. The reflective lenses made Myron Foote look like a little bug.

He dropped heavily into the seat beside Valerie.

"I'm just here until the coast is clear," Jack said.

His wife looked over at him with an inquisitive expression.

"Having a tough day, are we? Who's the little guy?"

"Oh, just someone who noticed that things aren't as they really should be. I wasn't completely truthful with him. And, some of the questions he asked, I didn't have the answers for anyway."

"Making any progress?" Val asked.

"Not yet. Myron Foote—that's his name—sort of ambushed me.

"We're not at the end of this trip yet. I've got to find some answers and hopefully track down a murderer. Feel free to stop me if you get a flash of inspiration."

"Well, I'm sure you'll get it all sorted out before too long. But, let me assure you, Mister. Once this train arrives at the station, I'm putting you under citizen's arrest. You'll come quietly and we are going to spend the rest of our holiday actually vacationing. Do you understand your rights?"

"Yes, officer."

Toulouse Gravelle was sitting by himself again. It seemed that Judge William Marshall had more business to transact than any retired person should reasonably have.

Jack could see him standing in the vestibule of the coach, speaking into his cell phone with great animation.

Maybe he does speaking engagements, Jack thought. *Could be he has to change his schedule because of this delay.*

"Sit down, Monsieur Jack. I want to talk to you," Gravelle said as Jack came toward him.

"Good afternoon, Mr. Gravelle. How is your afternoon going?"

"*Lentement.* Slowly. Please. Call me Luce."

Jack nodded.

Gravelle continued. "Look out that window. It is progressing slowly, right now. I didn't pay for this delay."

"Hopefully we'll be moving more quickly soon, though." Jack tried to sound encouraging.

"I've been thinking as I sit here," Gravelle said.

"About what?"

"I've heard quite a bit about my traveling companion, Judge Marshall. I always thought that some of his reputation depended on inflated stories of his adventures on the bench. But, now that I've had a chance to talk to him, I'm starting to believe he is as colorful as people have made him out to be."

"I've heard the stories too," Jack said. "So, he's not simply a man of legend but just as big in real life?"

"I had a chance to talk to him last night. And then today, since all this happened." He waved his hand around in a wide arc, to indicate the environment of the coach.

"He has told me more about his opinions on crime

and punishment," Gravelle continued. "He strikes me as a man I would not want to be on the bad side of."

"Well, he certainly has some strong opinions," Jack said.

"Last night he told me that he was upset with the state of the justice system. Well, you were there. You heard some of it too."

"Some of it? You mean there was more?"

"Lots more," Gravelle said. "He told me he thought it would be in the best interest of society if someone took up the task of administering justice to those who escaped severe punishment for the crime of which they were convicted."

"Really," Jack said. "But surely it was just the reaction of an old man who has spent much of his life looking at crime day after day. You don't think he was serious?"

"I'm not sure anymore, *mon ami.* He said he thought it would be a good thing if we tracked down people who had been given light sentences for major crimes and gave them what he called 'the ultimate punishment.' I think he really thinks we should establish some sort of vigilante justice."

"Sounds like the Wild West to me," Jack said.

"Look out the window," Gravelle said. "What is it, if not the Wild West?"

"You know what I mean. We're past the days when folks could take the law into their own hands, don't you think?"

"Do you read the newspapers, Jack? I challenge you

to read the news, any day of the week, and tell me that you truly believe people no longer take the law into their own hands. Just because a person is an officer of the courts does not make them immune from the desire for revenge."

"I suppose," Jack said. "But what makes you think William Marshall is having treacherous thoughts?"

"When we were talking last night, he was saying things like this," Gravelle said.

"He said, without any indication that he doubted his own words, 'While I was on the bench, I couldn't do anything about it. I had to work. And most of the time these guys went far away after getting off, or getting away lightly. But now that I'm retired, I can go where they are. I've got a few people in my sights already.' "

Jack was dumbfounded.

Gravelle continued. "Now, I don't know about you, but I'd want to give a wide berth to someone with those kinds of thoughts."

"Me too," Jack said. "Didn't give you any clue about who he was talking about, I don't suppose?"

"No. Not one."

"I think I'd like to talk to the man. I wouldn't want someone as highly respected as he was doing something foolish. For now, I've got other matters to deal with, though."

"Are you making any progress?" Gravelle asked.

"Just a little. I've got a theory about why our friend was killed, but no one I've spoken to strikes me as the culprit. A lot of folks are less than sympathetic about his leaving us as he did."

"Yeah. Marshall was one of them."

"I was one of whom?"

The voice was that of William Marshall. The judge had obviously completed his phone call and was now standing in the aisle, beside Jack and Toulouse Gravelle.

Jack could see the look of embarrassment on the politician's face. On the other side, the questioning expression on Marshall's face was evident.

Jack decided that the best course of action was to approach the subject head-on.

"We were discussing your stance in regard to the state of the court system these days. You've already told us that you feel that the penalties have been made too lax."

The judge roared with laughter in his inimitable way.

"Gravelle, would you mind terribly leaving this man and me alone for a few moments?" the judge asked. "We need to talk about serious matters. If you don't mind standing in the aisle, I don't mind if you stay, but you may be there for a little while."

"I will find another seat. I don't mind at all," Gravelle said, and gave a little bow.

From the tone of his voice and the look of disgust on the politician's face, Jack did not doubt he was telling the truth.

"Now," the judge began, once the politician had moved on, "let's talk about my experiences with the legal system."

"Gravelle was telling me," Jack said, "that you had an interesting time discussing the present state of the legal system."

"Son, let me tell you about what I think," the judge said. "I'm not sure that it is the fault of people who adjudicate the trials today. Their hands are tied by the way the laws have been changed.

"When I was on the bench, it was an eye for an eye and a tooth for a tooth and all that. If you came before me and your actions had resulted in the unjust death of another, and a lawyer could prove it, you would have to surrender your own life."

"You're still in favor of capital punishment," Jack said. "You've made that clear."

"You learn fast, son. Now, as I was saying, it's not the fault of the judges. They are doing what they can. I can't even blame the defense lawyers. Their job is to get their clients off. Problem is, there are now so many loopholes in the law that they can pretty much play that game and win a lesser sentence. The law lets it happen."

"But, even allowing for that, you would consider overriding a judicial decision and taking matters into your own hands?" Jack asked.

"Jack, there was a time when jail time meant spending time in a facility that reminded you, day after day, that you were being punished. Then the bleeding heart human rights folks came along and started talking up this cruel and unusual punishment stuff. Poor Bruiser has to sleep on a metal cot in a cell with three other guys. He's got bars on the door and has no personal privacy. Well, I don't buy that argument. You do criminal things, you get a criminal's reward, by my way of thinking. And that includes capital punishment for taking someone's life."

"Ever had the desire to mete out some justice of your own, now that you are off the bench?" Jack asked. "That would concern me greatly. I'd hate to see you defame yourself just because you disagree with the course of justice."

"While I was still on the bench, changes already had begun to take place." Marshall said. "I wasn't always happy with what I had to do, and I could sense the disappointment of those who were hoping that the ones who had hurt them would have to pay a price commensurate with their crime. It made me angry. There were times I wanted to come down from the bench and strangle someone who had devastated a whole family. But I didn't. I was an officer of the law. Justice must take its course, we've always been taught."

Jack pressed the issue.

"What about now? You're a private citizen. You can express an opinion about the law and challenge it more openly, at least as long as you stay within the law."

"Jack, if I were to commit a crime against another, I would expect that the law would mete out justice against me. I'm a religious man, of sorts. I believe that if the law failed, God would likely get me, one way or another. It's the way things should work. The law has to apply equally to everyone. I like that kind of balance."

"Well, Judge Marshall, I can't say that I agree with you," Jack said. "I guess I've been brought up in what some would call a more enlightened age. I'm satisfied that, for the most part, we have the best justice system there is, here in North America."

"I appreciate your candor, son. And I won't try to sway you. One of us is surely right. Time will tell who."

"Let me change the subject somewhat," Jack said.

"Fire away," the judge replied.

"What about Oscar Dempster? You don't think he was murdered? You challenged me earlier today, when we were talking with Gravelle."

"Never said that. I didn't share my opinion. I said *you* thought somebody done him in. We got talking about Broadway musicals before we could get into the subject. Remember?"

"So?" Jack said.

"So, I agree with your assessment. He was murdered. The culprit will be found and brought to justice in due course."

"That's a pretty bold assertion. You think we'll find out who did this before we arrive in Calgary?"

"I know you now, Jack. I know how you work. I can pretty much guarantee that you will figure this out before our journey ends."

"Wow! Thanks for the vote of confidence."

"I trust you to do the right thing, Jack," Judge Marshall replied.

"Got any advice?" Jack asked.

"You would do well to track down that young cop who has been on the train since this morning. He should be some help."

Jack almost laughed at the suggestion, but he didn't want to offend the poor old judge.

"I'm not so sure how much help he could give," Jack said. "He hasn't really been participating in the investigation quite as much as I might have expected."

"Sometimes it's just a matter of asking the right questions and drawing the right conclusions," the judge said, smiling amiably. "Now, if you'll excuse me I have to make a phone call."

With that, Judge William Marshall stood up and walked slowly to the end of the coach.

Jack watched as the man struggled with the door and entered the vestibule. The sound of the rails grew briefly louder, until the door closed.

Chapter Sixteen

If the judge only knew how much I hated trying to interact with that cop, he never would have suggested such a thing.

Jack made his way into the next coach, regretting that he had acted on the aged jurist's suggestion.

Roast, so far, had seemed self-absorbed and more intent on getting the trip over with than doing the job of policing.

The private eye was having serious doubts about the value of any further encounters.

Marshall must know something of Roast's expertise that has escaped me, Jack thought. *Oh, well. Nothing ventured. Nothing gained. I've got no other leads. Might as well make nice and see where it leads.*

The police officer was gazing out at the slowly passing scenery, as before, when Jack approached once again.

"Enjoying the view?" he asked, as he sat down beside Officer Roast.

"It has a certain hypnotic effect. Not a lot to see when you're going through the forests or riding the shores of a river. Every now and then, though, there is something to draw your attention and snap you out of your trance. I guess I can confess to enjoying it. How about you? Or are you still on the trail of your phantom?"

"Oh, I don't think it's a phantom. I believe there is a very real, flesh-and-blood murderer lurking."

"But you're not much closer. Do I have that right?" the officer asked.

"I think I'm traveling through a sort of mental forest, in the same way this coach is traversing that woodland outside the window. I know I'm moving toward my goal, but I can't tell from the landmarks, how close I am to my final destination."

Officer Roast nodded and continued to survey the countryside.

"I've been talking to the judge," Jack said. "He tells me you might be able to help."

Roast turned from the window to face Jack.

"What could I possible know that would help you in this case? I can't even say that you have a case."

Can't or won't, Jack wondered. "That was my initial reaction, when he made the suggestion," he said. "I figured it was worth a try."

"You really need to relax," Roast said. "You need to think happy thoughts for a while and stop obsessing about Oscar Dempster."

A thought made a fleeting journey across the investigator's mind. Jack filed it away with all the other things that were swirling around in his head.

"Let's pick up where we left off then," he said. "I'm sort of intrigued by the story you were telling about your family. I'd like to hear more."

"Not a lot to tell," Roast said.

"Well, what about your family? You got any kids?"

"Never had any. Never wanted any. At least, my wife didn't want any. Like I said before, she had some personal issues."

"I see," Jack said, though he didn't really know what the officer meant.

But it looked as if his companion wanted to talk.

"You know," Roast said, "I think she's afraid she might be *too* good at it."

"Now that's an interesting comment," Jack said.

"She went into police work to please her father. That was her initial motivation. Pop was a lawyer. She wanted to work for the law as well but didn't like what she saw the legal profession was doing to Dad."

"Was it causing her father to doubt his calling?" Jack asked.

"No. Quite the contrary. It was turning him into a tenacious fighter who wouldn't let go until, he felt, justice had been properly served. It was destroying their family."

Roast took a breath, appeared to consider what he should say next and continued.

"The issue had to do with her brother."

Jack just nodded encouragement and remained silent, hoping Roast would clear up the fog he felt he was trying to get through.

"Her brother was killed. A man in a stolen car, running from the cops, lost control, ran over the sidewalk, and pinned Junior against a tree.

"The medics came soon enough. It was just minutes, to hear her tell the story. They did the best they could, but he didn't make it."

Jack nodded. He could sense the anguish in the officer's voice. It crossed his mind that Roast was getting overly emotional, but he let it pass.

"The whole family was just so terribly broken up, emotionally, by the tragedy. Her dad seemed to take it hardest of all. He lived for that boy. There wasn't anything he wouldn't do for him. He envisioned a wonderful future for his son.

"Being a lawyer, he knew what the penalties were for that sort of crime. He was expecting that his son's killer would receive his due. I really think he expected that his friends in the fellowship of lawyers would make sure that the guy got the maximum penalty."

"Excuse me for interrupting," Jack said. "But, I assume that didn't happen the way your father-in-law had hoped."

"You've got that right," Roast said emphatically, anger blazing in his eyes. "The guy's lawyer dealt him down to manslaughter, and the jury chose to give him the minimum. It was just devastating to the family. I, sort of, think that my wife is so afraid of losing a child that she just doesn't want to think about having a family. I've grown to accept the fact.

"I'd love to have kids, but I love her too much to open the possibility of emotional trauma and fear for the future."

"I don't suppose you two have considered counseling to deal with the fears?" Jack asked.

"No. At least not yet."

"What about Dad?"

"He never gave up trying to get the sentence changed. But, it was no use. The courts weren't open to an appeal. He kept at it, though, until his career as a lawyer came to an end."

"That is truly sad," Jack said. "I am so sorry to hear such a tragic story."

"That's the way life is sometimes," Roast said. "You win some. You lose some. And some end in a draw. I think this one might be a draw."

Jack wasn't sure he understood what that meant, but he felt, now, that at least he had a little more insight into the life of the man that circumstance had brought across his path, earlier in the day.

The two men sat in silence as the train moved slowly toward its destination.

Jack Elton's mind was racing. Time was running short. And then a file drawer opened in his fatigued brain, and he knew he needed to talk to Stewart and arrange another trip to the computer room.

As Jack made his way down the aisle of the coach that Stewart had in his charge, he felt a tug at his sleeve.

When he looked down, the soft, wrinkled face of Ruby Dempster looked back.

"Sit down," she said quietly. "I need to talk."

"I'm sort of in the middle of something right now. Perhaps my wife, Valerie, could come back and join you."

"Sit down, young man. I know what you are doing. It is you I need to talk to."

Jack did as he had been told. He waited for the widow to speak.

"I know what you have been doing since early this morning," Ruby said. "I'm not blind, and I'm certainly not deaf. You don't think Oscar killed himself, do you?"

Jack was caught off guard by the woman's candor. There was a determination in her eyes that appeared to be a warning that he had best not try to lie.

"Well, Mrs. Dempster . . ."

"Call me Ruby. We're past the point where we need to stand on formality. Besides, from what I've heard, you prefer to call me by my first name anyway."

"Okay, Ruby, I've been known to look at situations with a more critical eye than some. I believe that, no, your husband did not kill himself."

"See? That didn't hurt, did it?" The woman gave a weak smile and continued. "I knew from the moment

I saw poor Oscar sitting on the floor with that horrible rope around his neck that it wasn't his handiwork."

"I see." That was all Jack could manage.

"You see, for all his bluster, he was a weak man. He covered well by making others feel small and ranting about the things that upset him. He didn't dare show anyone his fear. He didn't think it was a manly trait."

He sure had me fooled, Jack thought.

"As you may have gathered, he liked to gamble. Now, I can't say much about his past addiction. And I would have to confess that there have been times when he couldn't completely account for his whereabouts. I've always worried that he might build up some sort of gambling debt, and I'd have to open the door to some big burly man intent on throttling the man I've loved for almost fifty years. I found it best not to ask too many questions. I think it had something to do with his anger or his poker playing.

"So, Jack—I hope you don't mind me calling you Jack—stop trying to shield me from the truth. I know that Oscar didn't commit suicide. I know you've been looking for his killer. And I want to thank you for that. I'm relieved, but only a little, you understand, that he had not despaired of life to the point of wanting to end it himself."

"I just want to say how sorry I am you have to endure this at a time when you were hoping to celebrate your life together," Jack said. "I hope that those of us who are trying to help sort this out will be able to bring you some closure."

"Thank you, Jack," the widow said quietly.

She pulled a hanky from her sleeve and dabbed her eyes.

Jack stood and made signs to Valerie to keep an eye on Ruby. She gave him a nod and blew him a kiss, before sliding out of her seat.

Jack turned and headed toward the front of the coach. On his way, he noticed that the Guthries were watching him.

Greg Guthrie gave a nod, extended his hand, and wiggled his fingers in greeting. Hannah smiled and returned to a needlepoint she had been working on.

Jack made a mental note to get back to them later and try out the medical student's theory that there might be some truth hidden in their fantastic story of alien abduction, and ethereal voices.

Stewart was tidying up in his little cubicle near the front of the coach. Jack had evidently missed one of the afternoon snack services.

"Can you get me back into the computer room?" Jack asked. "I've got some research I'd like to do. I need to verify some facts and confirm a story or two. I don't know whether it will lead to anything, but at this point I'm willing to grasp at straws."

"I'm sure that won't be a problem, Jack. I think, with all the time this delay has added to our trip, the guys probably have most of their work done. You head on down. I'll radio ahead and let them know to expect you."

"Thanks," Jack said, as he turned and retraced his

path to the rear of the coach and the door leading out to the car that housed the communications center.

Stewart had been right. The room was empty. The computer was on. The screen saver showed the familiar Windows XP logo. It would appear in one corner of the black screen, disappear, and then reappear at another location.

Jack moved the mouse, and the desktop appeared. He opened the Internet browser and began his search.

He was soon engrossed in the process and had discovered that more information was to be had by those who had money to spend on getting the details he was looking for. He felt fortunate to discover that there were others who made it a hobby to deal with the same material. He joined a chat group and typed his question into a forum.

Any answer he might get back would depend on the frequency with which his fellow members visited the site and the availability of certain records for which he was looking.

Next he visited a government site, in search of information about one of his fellow passengers. He discovered what he was looking for in the archives.

As he sat and scanned the screen, another possible source of information crossed his mind. He switched to an online e-mail site and sent a message to an old friend. He marked it highest priority and prayed that the recipient would notice the flag before they left for home. He calculated the time difference between British Columbia and Ontario. There was still a chance.

When Jack checked back in the forum he had joined, there were still no replies to his inquiry.

This may be tougher than it looks. Better move on for now, and check back later.

Dave Cooke was in one of the little office spaces farther down the coach. Jack knocked gently on the door frame.

The man swiveled around in the chair he was using by the desk. His immediate look of recognition gave Jack the confidence to ask for permission to return later, in hopes of retrieving some valuable electronic data. At least, Jack hoped that something would await him, before it was too late, and that it would prove to be of value.

"Sure. Not a problem," Cooke said. "Stewart has vouched for you. That's good enough for me. If I'm not around, just go on in and do your thing."

The man gave Jack a smile and then swiveled back to his desk.

Jack figured he had just enough time to have a chat with the Guthries before he would have to make his return trip to the communications room.

Hannah Guthrie was still focused intently on making little cotton crosses with colored thread on the canvas spread over her lap. When she finished, some time in the distant future by Jack's estimation, it would be a rather large picture of a farmhouse, complete with a veranda and a sleeping hound dog.

Greg Guthrie was spread lazily over his side of the seat, looking out the window.

His relaxed posture brought his line of vision to just above the windowsill. He wasn't viewing much from his present position.

"Hi there," Jack said, stopping by the arm of Hannah's aisle seat.

"Hi," she said, and returned, immediately, to her cross-stitching.

Greg roused and pulled himself into a more upright posture.

"Hi there. How's it going?" the young man asked.

"I was just wondering if I could ask you folks a few questions," Jack replied, trying to sound upbeat.

"Sure, go ahead. What would you like to know?" Greg asked.

"You were talking earlier about your suspicions in regard to Mr. Dempster's death. You mentioned that you suspected some sort of alien involvement."

Jack could not believe he was getting into this sort of conversation willingly. But maybe there was something behind the Guthries' interpretation of events that held some truth.

It was a stretch, Jack had to admit. If nothing else, it promised to be entertaining.

Farther down the coach, he could see the young woman who had put him up to this. She was still folded up, watching the passing countryside.

Greg Guthrie's voice drew Jack's attention back to the couple sitting next to where he stood.

"Yeah. I heard voices. Kinda far-off voices. Sorta mechanical, if you know what I mean. Couldn't make out what they were saying. Funny, though, I thought I heard the theme from *Star Trek* just before the voices. It was back there, by the door." He indicated the back of the coach, by the washroom where Oscar Dempster had been found.

"I was just too scared to turn around and look. I was afraid of what I might see there."

"How about you, Hannah?" Jack asked. "Do you have anything to add?"

"Well, you know, I do remember hearing some sort of music. Now, I'm not as much a fan of those space shows as Greggie is. I couldn't tell you what music it was. Didn't last long at all. Hardly made an impression. I probably wouldn't have remembered it if Greg hadn't mentioned it, just now. But those voices? I didn't hear any of it."

If there is any reality in this, I'm sure not picking up on it, Jack thought. *Maybe my new Argentine friend has it all wrong.*

He turned toward the young man. *I can't believe I'm about to do this,* he thought, but decided to press on. "Tell me about the voices you heard."

"Thanks!" Greg said.

"Sorry?" Jack said, confused by the response.

"A lot of folks don't ask for more information when I tell them about stuff."

"Well, to be honest, it's only certain 'stuff' I'm interested in, Greg. And those voices intrigue me. Tell me more."

Greg Guthrie looked happy to oblige, and Jack knew he would have to be careful to guide the young man's response so that the explanation didn't take the rest of the trip.

The young man wound up for the pitch.

"Well, first off, there was the music. It was *Star Trek* for sure. Not loud. I mean, not eight-channel surround sound loud, but I could hear it well enough not to mistake it. Loud enough to be heard over the sound of the train. You know, I've always enjoyed—"

"Perhaps you could get to the voices," Jack interjected. "I'm sort of under the pressure of time here."

"Oh, yeah. Sorry. Well, after the music, I heard voices. One was clearer than the other."

"Two voices?" Jack asked.

"Pretty sure it was only two. Like I said, one was clearer than the other. Sounded close by, but I couldn't tell what was being said. The other one sounded like it was coming from, you know, outer space, like. Kind of tinny, like someone talking into the end of a soup can. You know, when I was younger, my brother and I used to make a telephone with tin cans. We'd punch a hole in the bottom and then—"

"You couldn't tell anything that was being said?" Jack interrupted.

"Well, it depended on how tight the string was. You needed to pull the cans—"

"I meant the voices you heard on the train."

This was getting harder than it looked.

"Oh, I see," Greg said. "No. Couldn't pick anything out. Course, I wasn't trying to eavesdrop. Liked that music though. Another one I like is—"

"So, it always happened the same way? *Star Trek*, then the voices?

"Always. Then it would seem the clearer voice would speak first. Sort of a grunt."

"I see," Jack said. "Did you notice anything else?"

Both Greg and Hannah shook their heads.

"Nope. Nothing out of the ordinary," the young man said.

Jack tried hard not to smile.

"Thanks, folks. You've given me a lot to think about. I'm sure we'll talk again before our trip is through. I'll be going now," Jack said.

He fled down the coach and out into the all-encompassing roar between the rail cars. He had an idea—maybe an explanation. He was going to have to dig a little deeper.

Jack leaned on the crash bar of the door into the next coach and moved into the relative quiet of the rail car. He made his way to the communications center to look for answers to his inquiries. He was not to be disappointed.

Chapter Seventeen

When Jack opened the e-mail folder, he discovered that his friend from Ontario, Jim Linden, had been able to find some of the information the investigator had requested.

Hi, Jack. You caught me just as I was headed out the door for dinner. Ruth and I are meeting at a little restaurant in town. No special reason. Just to make up for all the dinners I miss doing office stuff. LOL

Sounds like you've got your hands full. BTW, congrats on the wedding. Val sounds like a great gal.

Anyway, I checked out your guy. He was trained here at the police college and did fairly well in most things. Really good with a gun. Don't get him angry. LOL

Left here after graduating. Went out west. Had a few problems and was dismissed from the force in Alberta. Last we have, he was second-in-command at a little place over in your neck of the woods. Lives there with his wife. She was a graduate from here too.

I got something else that I think you might be able to use to advantage. Don't want to write it. You'll have to call me. Sensitive stuff. You might want to ask questions.

I'll have my cell phone on.

The police instructor, who had been one of Jack's mentors more years ago now than he cared to count, gave his phone number and signed off his letter.

Jack printed the message, erased it from the computer, and went in search of a response in the forum he had joined on a genealogy site. It wasn't lineages he needed to know so much. He was tracking marriage records and death notices. He was working on a hunch but was completely unsure whether he would turn anything up.

There were nine responses to his query. None of them very helpful.

Because of the concern for privacy and the protection of personal information, Jack was not surprised to learn that there was not a lot of material readily available to the public. Some information could be retrieved if it was more than forty years old. Other records, as he had already determined, could only be acquired for a fee. In most cases, you were also asked to prove your need to know.

Everyone was extremely apologetic. Most of the respondents sympathized with Jack's plight. They had had the same problems just trying to track down records for their own ancestors. It was evident that their hobby was time consuming and, sometimes, expensive.

Jack hoped that his friend, Jim Linden, had some good information to help with the solution to Oscar Dempster's untimely demise.

He realized immediately that he was facing a major problem. He had not brought his cell phone on the trip. Val had left hers behind as well, reasoning that if they were supposed to be on vacation, alone, they didn't need any intrusions. And they didn't need the temptation to be communicating with the outside world. The hope had been that they would travel around, in a protective bubble of anonymity, and enjoy their honeymoon.

I guess that plan has gone by the wayside, for now at least, Jack thought.

There was communications gear on the train, but it was reserved for company business and strict emergencies. Jack thought, momentarily, about pressing his case with Dave Cooke but remembered that there were at least two other people on the trip who had cell phones that seemed to work. With the train approaching the city, the signal would become more certain with the passage of time.

Jack decided to talk to Judge Marshall. Surely the jurist would want to help with the solution to the puzzle.

As if to confirm the wisdom of his decision, when the private investigator opened the door to the platform between the coaches, he was greeted not only by the sounds of the train, the rush of the wind, and the odors that only rail travel can conjure, but by the smiling countenance of Judge William Marshall.

The man was just finishing up his conversation when he saw Jack. He nodded, said a few closing words, and snapped the phone shut.

Jack indicated, by pointing, that he wanted to speak to Marshall in the quieter environment beyond the door.

The two moved into the coach. Jack held the door for the older man.

"How's it going, son?" the judge asked. "Making any progress? I'm sure you'll figure this all out before long."

"I sure hope so," Jack said. "Time is getting tight. I think I'm making a little progress, but I need your help."

The judge's eyebrows rose and a broad smile came over his face. He looked ready to pour out his accumulated legal knowledge, right there in the middle of the tourist-class coach.

"Ah, I knew it would come to this. I'll do what I can. What would you like to know?"

"It's not quite like that, Judge Marshall. I'm looking for a phone," Jack said. "I need to call someone. I noticed that you have one. Could I possibly borrow it? I'll pay you whatever you think the call might cost."

"Couple of things, son. It's William, remember? Not Willie or Bill or Billy. Certainly not Judge Marshall. And, second, the call's free. We gotta work together on these things, son. I want to help you solve this. I've developed a personal interest in this case."

He reached into his jacket and pulled out the phone.

Handing it to Jack, the judge said, finally, "Just bring it back to me when you're done. We can talk some more. I want to see where you're at with this."

"Thanks. I won't be long," Jack said, as he took the device and fished in his shirt pocket for the e-mail with the phone number.

The private investigator found an empty seat and carefully dialed his friend's cell. The phone rang. It rang again. And then, "The subscriber you are calling is away from the phone or out of the calling area. Please hang up, and try again later."

The volume was so loud that he had to quickly move the phone away from his ear. One or two of the passengers looked up from whatever they were doing. The judge was obviously losing his hearing.

Jim must still be on the road, Jack thought.

His friend, besides teaching in the classroom, also taught defensive driving to his students. His pet peeve was people who tried to drive and talk on a cell phone at the same time. He'd seen his share of accidents caused by inattentiveness and taught his students to convey that message to others.

"You officers are going to have enough distractions

in your job. Because you need to be communicating, you'll have to do two things at once, sometimes, out of necessity. Use hands-free when you can. Keep both hands on the wheel, and pay attention. When you're not enroute to something, or in pursuit, pull over to talk."

Jim Linden's words of advice still echoed in Jack's memory, from a visit he had made to his mentor at the police college a few years earlier. Jim practiced what he preached. His cell phone was off whenever he got behind the wheel.

Jack checked his watch and then the view from the window. Another hour, or two, and the *Last Spike Special* would be in the station. There was the chance that, if he didn't come up with some answers to share with the investigators who would board the coach upon their arrival, a lot of angry patrons would be sitting and waiting to be allowed their freedom, while the police looked for clues and asked all their questions.

I sure hope Judge Marshall is right about being able to figure this out, he thought.

Jack walked down the aisle of the coach to where Judge Marshall had resumed his seat next to Gravelle. He handed him back the phone.

"My party is not available right now. May I borrow this a little later?" he asked.

Marshall handed the device back.

"Hang on to it, son. I don't need it right now. You make your connection first. No big rush. Neither you nor I are going to be far apart for the next while."

Jack took the phone again and adjusted the volume. The phone beeped more and more quietly. A graph on the screen also indicated that the sound level was being reduced. The judge saw what he was doing.

"Oops, sorry. I should have mentioned that before now. My hearing's not as good as it used to be, and with the sound of the train, it's even worse. Feel free to make it comfortable for you. I can adjust it later, if I need to."

Jack was still standing in the aisle.

The judge leaned over toward him. He looked up and asked, "Did ya get anything new from Officer Charles?"

"We talked about his family a little. I gather his wife and her family have gone through some tough times."

The judge nodded as Jack spoke.

"I didn't get much satisfaction as far as the present case is concerned, though," Jack said.

"Maybe you're not asking the right questions," Marshall said with a smile and a slight shake of the head.

"Well, I tried. He didn't seem to be in an answering mood, at least as far as Oscar Dempster is concerned."

The judge did not reply. He just made a tent in front of his mouth with his fingers and stared straight ahead.

"Maybe you should try your call again," the jurist suggested.

"Thanks. I'll do that."

Jack moved out of hearing range of the other passengers and pressed REDIAL on the cell phone. He placed the receiver gingerly against his ear and tested the volume of the ringing at the other end of the line.

"Hello. That you Jack?" Jim Linden's voice asked.

"Yeah, it's me," Jack said.

"Listen, I'm just in the parking lot right now. I've got some stuff I need to read to you. Can I call you back in a couple of minutes?"

Jack agreed and asked his friend to stay on the line for a moment. He walked back to where Marshall was sitting.

"What's your cell number?" he asked.

The judge looked up, confused.

"My friend has to call me back. Can I have your cell number?"

Jack passed the number along to Linden and promised he would stay ready for the return call. Then he retreated to the dome car to wait, while the Linden's were seated in a restaurant almost three thousand miles to the east. He put the phone in a pants pocket so his hands would be free to steady himself as he made the journey between coaches.

And then he waited, aware that the miles were shortening with each passing moment. Either the restaurant parking lot was very large or the Linden's were being forced to wait for an empty table.

The minutes dragged on. Jack watched as railway staff began the task of preparing the train for its arrival in the city. The process was begun early so that everyone could be in their places when the passengers disembarked. As well, the staff were beginning to tire and were anxious to get to their own accommodations in the hotel. They would need to rest for the return trip the next day.

When Jim Linden's call finally came, Jack was startled by the sound of the judge's ringtone. Confusing thoughts ran through his mind as he struggled to retrieve the phone and open it so he could talk with his friend.

"Hi Jack. Sorry about the delay. We got stuck at the reception desk, and there was no place to sit down.

"We've ordered, so I shouldn't be disturbed for a little while. Have you got some time to talk? Maybe I should have said 'listen.' "

Jack found a chair in one of the work rooms and sat down.

For the next ten minutes he listened, giving grunts of encouragement from time to time to let his friend know he was still at the other end of the line.

He retrieved Jim's e-mail again and made notes on the back of the sheet, as his friend told him what he had discovered.

Jack had heard some of this before, from a different perspective, but Jim Linden was filling in some important blanks for him.

"So, Jack, is any of this going to be any help to you?" the police instructor asked.

"I'm almost certain it is. Strange, isn't it, how circumstances can bring people together and have the power to both unite and to cause division? This certainly narrows the field of suspects."

"Have you got enough time to do anything before you reach the station?"

"All I can do is hope," Jack replied. "And try to move as quickly as I can. We don't want someone to get away with murder tonight."

"Well, good luck. My steak is here. Let me know how this all turns out, will ya."

"Sure thing. And, Jim . . ."

"Yeah. What, buddy?"

"Thanks for this. You've made my day—I think."

"Go get 'em," Linden said.

The line went dead.

Jack returned to the coach where Oscar Dempster had died. He was reflecting on the call as he went. Not only had he been given valuable information, but his friend had inadvertently solved another puzzle.

Jack hummed as he walked. It was the ringtone from the judge's phone. He marveled at how modern digital technology made it possible to have your cell phone alert you with high quality tunes.

Marshall's ringtone sounded like a high-pitched female voice. It was a haunting melody, without words. It was recognizable to anyone who had grown up in front of a television set in the late sixties, and beyond.

When Jim Linden called, Jack had been alerted by an exact rendition of the theme music from *Star Trek*.

Chapter Eighteen

Jack now had the answer to the question about what the Guthries might have heard earlier in the day. It had been the ringing of Judge Marshall's phone. When Marshall had answered, the Guthries had heard what they thought were alien communications. It had actually been the result of his turning up the volume to compensate for his failing hearing.

That was the end of that mystery, as far as the private investigator was concerned. Time to move on to more important pursuits.

"That's an interesting ringtone you have, Judge—I mean William. It caught me right off guard. Amazing what they can do in such a small space these days."

"Sorry 'bout that, son. It's a hobby of mine, sort of. I got caught up in that program when it first came on

TV. I've followed the series since then. Been to all the movies too. Can't say I've been to a convention. Not sure I'd feel comfortable. I'm not as young as I used to be and would probably look foolish in a Captain Kirk getup."

The old gentleman patted his protruding belly and laughed his trademark laugh.

"I'm sure you'd fit in just fine," Jack said. "I don't think they would require you to show up in uniform or to wear pointy Mr. Spock ears."

"Maybe I could wear my old bench robes and be some sort of alien."

"I think the black robe thing belongs to Darth Vader. That's a whole other story," Jack replied, with a smile.

"So, how's the investigation coming along?" the judge asked, apparently tiring of the discussion of his personal hobby.

"I'm a lot closer now than I was half an hour ago," Jack replied. "I've got more than one person to question, before this day is over."

"Well, get on with it, son. Time's a wastin'. I'll be right here, if you need me.

"That's encouraging," Jack said. "I'll be back."

He headed down the coach toward the first person who caught his attention.

The medical student, Nadia, was gazing out the window.

As the train approached a more civilized part of the province, there were farms scattered beside the tracks.

Vast acreages that had meant prosperity for the early Canadian West spread for what seemed like miles from the tracks.

A single house, surrounded by outbuildings, sat in the midst of each huge tract of land.

The fields were populated by herds of docile cattle that would eventually find their way to the dinner tables of carnivorous North Americans.

Some of the animals lay in the fields. Others stood, watching the train pass, slowly chewing on bits of straw and grass and unmoved by the metallic snake that was wending its way through their domain.

The girl looked up as Jack approached. A broad smile blossomed on her face.

"Hello, my friend. *Que pasa?* What's happening?"

"Well, for one thing, you were right about my new friends, the Guthries. I still don't believe their story about the overtaking of the world by aliens, but they were right about the voices. You didn't hear the other clue that they gave me. It pretty much helped to solve the mystery. They said they heard the theme song of a space show we used to have here, in North America.

"Well, the judge was using the music for the ring-tone on his cell phone. Someone called him this morning. That's when they heard it."

Jack lowered his voice before sharing his next little tidbit, though, on reflection, he realized that it would not have been heard by the judge.

"He turned his phone volume way up high, 'cause

he's hard of hearing. Those were the voices they thought they heard."

Nadia covered her mouth and giggled at this revelation.

"And your investigation?" she asked.

"I still have some loose ends to tie up. A nice clean confession from someone would go a long way to easing my frustrations. Got any truth serum on you?"

"I think, my friend, you are on your own with this one. I suggest you get all your facts together and when— maybe I should say if—you get your suspect, confront the individual with those facts."

"Thanks," Jack said. "I'll remember that. Gotta keep moving. Enjoy the rest of your trip."

The girl turned again to staring out the window.

"You know," she said, as Jack began to move away, "We have many cattle in my country. Argentina is famous for its *carne,* its beef."

"I'd love to stay and talk about a nice thick steak, but I've got some folks I desperately need to talk with. See you later," Jack said, and moved along the aisle.

Stewart was sitting in one of the seats, filling out report forms, before the end of the trip.

Jack sat down beside him and waited for the attendant to finish what he was writing.

"I suppose you are going to have to fill in a lot more of those than usual this time," he said.

Stewart looked at his watch.

"It looks like I will be in the office until later this evening. I've never experienced anything like this, but even when someone is injured, the paperwork goes on and on. It's a liability thing. We have to demonstrate due diligence. Show that it wasn't our fault and be able to back that up for the insurance people and, I guess, the courts, if it were to come to that. I'm not looking forward to this at all."

"I want you to think back to this morning," Jack said. "Maybe I can make your job a little easier. I'll just need some more time."

"Sounds good. Do you really think you can do that?"

The man looked hopefully at the private investigator.

"Stewart, I'm going to ask you to try to remember everything that you can about the sequence of events earlier today. It is vital that we piece together as much as we can the events surrounding Mr. Dempster's death. What do you remember about this morning, from the time you boarded until his body was found?" Jack asked.

"Sir . . . um, Jack. I don't think I can be of much help. I was on the coach about half an hour before you guys arrived from the hotel. I was arranging things for the morning and reviewing my notes for the places of interest we were supposed to pass.

"The trainman usually keeps an eye out for the buses and radios us before they arrive at the platform, so we can be there to greet the passengers. I wasn't paying much attention to anything else until I got the call on my radio. I went to the door and put down the stool so folks didn't have such a distance to reach the first step of the coach. I stood on the platform and greeted everyone.

"Mr. and Mrs. Dempster looked tired, but happy, when they arrived. I guessed they had an exciting evening and enjoyed their time in the city. I didn't notice anything out of the ordinary."

"How about once we were on the coach?" Jack asked. "Anything strike you as unusual, or different, from other mornings?"

"To be frank with you, apart from making the announcements about the day's trip and telling folks that they were about to be fed again, I've got enough to keep me busy so that I don't notice a lot of what's going on, unless there's an emergency of some sort. I wasn't particularly watching the far end of the coach, although I do remember seeing Mr. Dempster heading that way with a sort of shaving kit. I assumed he was going to freshen up before breakfast. Some folks sleep in and don't get to do those things before they have to leave for the station."

"So, the next thing you noticed was Bob Benson yelling about the dead guy in the lavatory?" Jack asked.

"Yeah. That's about it. I'm sorry I'm not being much help."

"Okay. So, Bob Benson comes out, screaming like a banshee and running for his seat. You look up from what you're doing. Did you see anything unusual?"

"Other than Mr. Benson, nothing unusual. Mrs. Dempster was heading for the washroom to look. Your wife was following close behind. Folks were pretty much looking shocked, as you would expect. Judge Marshall had been talking on his cell phone and cut his conversation short, far as I can tell. He was quite helpful."

"How so?" Jack asked.

The two men talked a little longer before Jack made a move to leave the coach attendant's side.

"I may have another question or two for you shortly," Jack said. "I hope you will have the information you are going to need by the time we arrive at the station."

"Before we get there, I hope," the coach attendant said. "I'll have some talking to do before I get to the writing. I'd like to keep my superiors as calm as possible."

Jack promised to do his best and then began the return trip to the dome car.

On the way, he stopped to talk to Val.

"So, how is my husband and favorite investigator doing now?"

"I'm hoping that I'll be able to devote all of my time to vacationing with you before long," he said.

"Well, that's good. I'm hoping to get off once we reach the station. I'm sort of hoping you'll come along too."

"So am I," Jack said.

He looked at his watch once again. The pressure of time weighed heavily. The stress of the day was taking its toll.

One way or the other, I'll be done within the next hour, he thought.

He was thankful that Val had been as understanding as she' been. Because she was a police officer, she knew how these things could drag on and take up time away from friends and family. She probably hadn't expected that it would intrude into their honeymoon, though.

The thought entered Jack's mind, as once again, he walked to the front of the tourist-class coach, *Stewart is earning his pay today. I've got to ask for more details.*

As he passed the young couple, still sitting and looking as if they had been transplanted from the hippie culture of the mid-sixties, Greg Guthrie caught his eye and motioned him toward their seats, an excited look on his face.

"I heard the music again," he said, wide-eyed, when the private investigator responded to the frantic gestures.

"I'm not surprised," Jack said. "I had a suspicion that, if you paid attention, you would."

"So, it really is aliens?"

"Not quite, my man. But it is something out of the ordinary. Hang in there. I'm hoping I can give you a bit more information soon."

"Cool," Greg Guthrie replied, and sat back with a look of satisfaction on his face.

I'm not going to get into a debate about the alien abduction theory. The guy sure has helped more than he knows. I'll have to let him know, when this is over, Jack thought, as he resumed the journey to where Stewart was standing.

The coach attendant was methodically packing boxes with bags of prepackaged snacks. Partially filled cases of soft drinks stood against the wall, awaiting the reorganization of their contents. A number of large green bags were visible inside the doorway of Stewart's storage room.

Jack waited until the box that was presently being attended to was filled, and the flaps had been folded to make the contents secure.

Stewart rose from his squatting position using one hand to support himself on the armrest of one of the seats. The other hand went to his lower back and massaged, Jack supposed, tired and aching muscles.

"Me again," he said.

"So I see. Tell me, Jack, are you feeling as tired as I am at this point? Ya know, we advertise this trip as a relaxing vacation. Seems to me, you haven't really been getting your money's worth on this part of your journey."

"My wife tells me that if I didn't have something to do, Jack would probably be a very dull boy. I find this whole thing energizing, in a strange way. I don't know if you understand what I mean."

"Probably not," Stewart replied. "I do applaud your enthusiasm, though. If it were me, I'd be saying, let Jack do it."

At that point, a comical look came over the attendant's face, and he began to laugh.

Between fits of laughter, he managed to get out, "I guess that's what I did, didn't I? I let Jack do it, didn't I, Jack?"

When the humor of the comment finally struck Jack's tired brain, he was only able to give a weak smile at what was a rare moment of cheerfulness. He didn't have the heart to tell the coach attendant that it was 'George' who, according to the old saying, folks suggested should do it.

"I've got a few more questions, if you don't mind," Jack said, when the moment of jollity had subsided.

"Like I said before, I'll do what I can. Just forgive me if my mind is a little dull at this point."

The two men sat down. Stewart seemed supremely pleased to be able to rest for a moment.

"When Roast came on board, what did you say to him?" Jack asked, shifting in the seat so he could focus all of his attention on the man beside him.

"Let me see. I think I can still recall my exact words. There weren't many. He said hello and introduced himself. Showed his badge. I said, 'We have a man who has died. He is in the lavatory.' He said 'thanks,' and you pretty much know the rest."

"Wait a minute," Jack said. "Are you sure those were your exact words? You didn't say anything else to him?"

"No. I remember thinking about something I heard on TV a while ago, something about not volunteering information. The police have a procedure they follow and they don't like you to jump ahead."

"I'm not so sure that you have your facts straight on that one. But if you are sure about what you did say, I think we're on our way to a showdown of sorts. I'm going to need some help."

"I'll do what I can," Stewart said.

While Jack felt compassion for Stewart and knew the man could benefit from a few more moments of repose, the fact was that the train was moving toward its destination and an appointment with authorities who would want either an explanation or the valuable time of the folks on at least two of the coaches.

The picture was becoming much clearer, but there were a few more questions to be answered and, Jack knew, a murderer to be confronted. How that would play out was not at all certain.

He excused himself and went in search of Judge William Marshall. The man was not sitting where he had been left. While there were one or two other places where he could be, Jack was almost certain he knew where the jurist would be found.

The wind between the coaches blew warm on Jack's face. The sound of the steel wheels passing over the frogs—those places where parallel tracks intersected before separating again—added an occasional low rumble to the rhythmic sound of the coach passing over the joints in the ribbon of steel that led inexorably into the city that was its final destination for the day.

"This takes me back to my childhood," Judge Marshall

said over the noise, leaning out over the bottom half of the Dutch door of the coach exit. "We used to live right by the railroad tracks. That was back in the days of steam locomotives. You probably don't remember back that far, do you, son?"

"Oh, I wouldn't be too quick to draw that conclusion, sir. I can still remember the occasional steam-powered train from my youth."

"There you go, getting all formal again. Enough of that 'sir' stuff."

The judge continued. "I really regret not paying more attention to those things. There they were, those great smoking engines. They were a vital part of the history of the country. Steam locomotives before them had been responsible for opening up the land—opening up this very passageway that we're riding on today. Now you can only see 'em in museums or rotting away in a park somewhere. It's tragic, just tragic."

"Judge Marshall, we need to talk. Can we step inside?" Jack asked over the noise of wind and the rails.

"That's the second time now. All this formal stuff makes me think you've got something serious on your mind, son. Lead on. I'll be right behind you."

Once they were back inside the coach, Marshall turned toward Jack.

"Now, son, what's on your mind? Is it something to do with your suspicions about Oscar Dempster's death and your search for answers?"

"I have some interesting information that I'm going to want to discuss with you before we arrive in the city," Jack said. "I've been talking to a friend of mine back east. That's why I needed your phone."

"To do with the murder of Oscar Dempster, I suppose?"

"Yes, that," Jack said.

Considering what else had been revealed to him by Jim Linden, there were some other things he would also need to pursue with the judge.

"Let's sit down," Jack said. "This may take some time, and it would be best if we didn't waste what's left of the trip trying to keep upright."

As the train began its approach to the city, there were more and more switches to cross as it negotiated its way onto the track that would lead it into the terminal. Even at slow speed, some of the movement could be violent enough to cause the unwary to lose their balance.

Jack was aware of this and did not want the older man to be in worse jeopardy than he already was.

"Alright, Jack. Give me the benefit of your acute reasoning powers. What have you got to tell me?"

"Well, for one, I've got to tell you that I don't believe you have been on the level with me. I've discovered that you are well acquainted with the victim in this crime. I have every reason to believe that you are partly, if not wholly, to blame for Oscar Dempster's death."

"Well now, Jack," the judge said, "whether I am, or not, is up to a court of law, as you may well know. And, since I have not been charged, I guess I don't have to prove anything. You, on the other hand, have made some pretty strong accusations just now. I hope you have good reason to speak as you do and can defend your hypothesis."

"Are you denying that you knew Oscar Dempster and that you had anything to do with what happened today?" Jack asked.

"I'm about to give you the surprise of your life, young man. The answer to your question is that I am trying to do nothing of the sort. I am, however, a man of law, and I want to play out this little exercise of injustice to a fitting conclusion.

"You see, in spite of all you might think you know about me, about my background, about my relationship to Oscar Dempster, you don't know the whole story. I will shock you further, before this is over. But, for now, present your case."

"I think there is someone we need to talk to," Jack said.

Chapter Nineteen

Music was playing quietly in the dome car as Jack and Judge William Marshall ascended the stairs.

Progress was slow. The judge was showing the effects of advancing arthritis.

Jack was suddenly fatigued. He was beginning to feel as if he had walked the whole way from Vancouver. He pulled himself up the stair railing, hand over hand, and found himself somewhat winded once he reached the top.

Charles Roast was sitting in his usual place. He watched the coaches ahead as they snaked through the switch yard just outside the city.

To the left and right of the *Last Spike Special,* diesels on other tracks shuttled coaches and freight cars back and forth to make up the consists for trains that would head out later that evening or early the next morning.

The coach had more passengers, now that the scenery had become more interesting. The police officer sat by himself. He did not notice when the two other men approached.

"Me again," Jack said jovially as he stood beside the police officer. "You've been holding out on me. I thought we were going to do some bonding, be honest with one another."

"Hi, Chuck," Marshall said, and slid into the seat.

The man's head snapped around.

"Don't call me that. You know how I hate being called Chuck. I cannot believe that loving parents could do something like that to their child. I'll never forgive them for that. You don't like being called anything other than William or Judge Marshall or Sir. Well, I feel even worse, being known all my life as Chuck Roast. And you know it."

"Okay, *Charles*. This nice young man has found out some things about you and me. I think he has some things to tell us. He will probably threaten some sort of legal action. And I know he will have some questions. If he doesn't, I'll have some things to say that will make him ask a question or two.

"Go ahead, Jack," the jurist said, in a voice that threw down a challenging gauntlet. "What have you got?"

"Let's start with your relationship to one another," Jack said.

"Okay, lets," Roast said.

"Officer, you are this man's son-in-law. Your wife is

Heather Marshall, the judge's daughter. You met her while you were in training at the police college, in Ontario."

The other two men nodded their agreement.

"Judge Marshall—William—you wanted to know my evidence. To give that to you, I need to be very frank about what Charles has told me. He was very careful not to name names. And he omitted some details so that you would be protected. But now, I have to tell you what I know and what I believe."

"Seems reasonable to me," the judge said.

"You were making a name for yourself as a lawyer when your daughter, Heather, was looking at her options for her life's vocation."

"Yes. I was doing pretty well, even if I do say so myself. I was becoming known as a . . ."

"As a real fighter." Jack finished the sentence for him. "You wanted her to become a lawyer too. You were . . . how shall I put it? Rather forceful in expressing your wishes."

Marshall nodded.

"You were disappointed when Heather told you she did not want to end up like you. That was because, besides becoming a fighter in the courtroom, you had become a very angry man at home.

"You certainly took your work seriously. And you had a right, even an obligation, to fight for justice when a crime had been committed. But, you brought that spirit home with you. You were somewhat of a tyrant. Heather didn't like that. But she loved you nevertheless."

"I guess you're right," the judge said.

"Of course, he's right," Roast chimed in. "Carry on."

"And then your son was killed. It almost destroyed your career. Not just the pain of losing a child so sense-lessly, but also the stress of trying to bring the killer to justice just about tore you apart.

"The way Charles tells it, your son's killer was driving a stolen car, running from the police. He lost control, ran over the sidewalk, and pinned William Junior—you used to call him Billy—against a tree.

"Let me just say how sorry I am over your loss. I know that, even after all these years, you still mourn his death." Jack continued, "It was that event that set the course for Heather. She determined that she could ac-complish two things by becoming a police officer."

"What things?" Judge Marshall asked.

"She would help alleviate your frustration at not hav-ing a child follow you into law. She felt she could earn back some of your love and respect."

"And . . ."

"And she could be on the front lines, so to speak, to deal with others who might break the law and cause suffering to others. You see, you had instilled that in her—the desire to administer justice and to fight for the underdog."

"But what's this got to do with what happened this morning?" Roast asked.

"Both you and the judge know that it has everything to do with it. The young man who killed William

Junior was Oscar Dempster. Then, as now, he was prone to impulsive acts. He ended up on that sidewalk, never having intended to do anyone any harm. He was fleeing the law in a stolen car and, tragically, turned the wrong way.

"That's not to excuse him in any way. He deserved to be punished."

"Problem was, he wasn't punished, at least not to my satisfaction," Marshall said, anger apparent in his voice and countenance.

"He did spend some time in jail," Jack said.

"A stupid sentence. The man had killed my boy. Junior was going to become a lawyer. Murderers deserve to be put to death. I couldn't convince the prosecution of that. And the fool who took on his defense just went in and made a deal, so Dempster gets a manslaughter charge."

"It was about that time that you were made a judge," Jack said. "You were certainly in no position, by then, to do anything else about Oscar. So, you put your anger on a back burner and went on with your life and your career in law. Meanwhile, Heather had met up with a young, aspiring police cadet who shared her passion for justice. Interesting how justice can be perverted by our reaction to life's circumstances. I'll get to that."

"Heather and I fell in love almost at first sight," Roast said. "The fact that she shared my passion to serve and protect was just an added bonus."

"And, don't forget, you both shared a common experience," Jack said. "A drunk driver was responsible for the death of both your parents, Charles. Your little sister too. You were angry about that. Had every right to be. Judge Marshall was the one who handled that case. He told me so earlier today. It was, of course, before you and Heather met.

"How did you deal with that, William? It must have just about done you in, to let that fellow off."

The jurist shook his head sadly.

"I always took pride in respecting the law. I knew there was legislation in place to protect the innocent ones. And I knew that there were times when that same law might set the guilty free. It's the price you pay for trying to keep the courts honest.

"I knew the kid was roaring drunk the night he took those three innocent lives. Everyone knew it. But there had been some sort of foul-up in the paperwork, and there just wasn't any way out of that hole—not legally anyway. I had to let him go. He left town and dis- appeared. I guess he knew he had got off easily. I hope he made a fresh start—a sober one."

"So, this is what I've got so far," Jack said. "My friend, Jim Linden, tells me that Heather and Charles became an item and decided to spend their lives to- gether as husband and wife, fighting for truth, justice, and the North American way."

Jack looked at Roast.

"I can only assume that the two of you had, by then, put the painful experiences of the past behind you. At that point in your lives, they became simply the driving force that made you want to protect others from the anguish you had both felt. But there were other forces that brought you to today."

Charles Roast looked sadly at his father-in-law.

"I guess you're right," he said.

"Judge Marshall," Jack continued. "You can be a very convincing man. I suspect that you shared your pain, as well as your opinions, with Charles and Heather. I have no doubt that, because your anger about perceived miscarriages of justice had become a constant companion, you spoke about the sort of revenge you wished you could mete out to the likes of Oscar Dempster.

"They loved you, and they listened. And you eventually won them over to your way of thinking, at least as far as your plan was concerned."

"Not right away, Jack," the judge replied. "There was no plan to do anything until recently. But I'll have to admit that I could not let the anger go. And so, we find ourselves sitting on this luxurious train. We should be as happy as kings. But we're not, are we, Jack?"

The private investigator now turned to Roast.

"The three of you probably discussed various scenarios for what should happen to Dempster."

"That's about the way it was," the officer said. "Heather and I would go over to visit her dad. She'd cook dinner for him, after Ma Marshall died. That was before he moved in with us. We'd sit around the table and talk about how we could do someone in. We'd discuss possible ways to get away with it. Heather and I had been taught about ways, both legal and illegal, to immobilize someone. The judge knew the law. It started out as just talk. That's all I thought it would ever be. That's all I wanted it to be."

"But he convinced you, didn't he?" Jack said.

Officer Roast hung his head.

"Jack, you're doing a bang-up job of theorizing how we might be accomplices in the death of Oscar Dempster, but you're going to have to do better than that," Marshall said. "Yes, we . . . perhaps I should say, *I* have a motive for wanting to see Oscar Dempster out of the way. But, I'll bet if you asked most of the folks who experienced that man, yesterday, you'll find plenty of motives for murder."

Jack could not deny the truth of that statement, but the judge had as much as admitted to the deed.

"For a while, there, you sounded like you wanted to be proven guilty," Jack said.

"You may be right. You'll find, if you haven't already, that I am a rather strange bird. What I say, I mean. What's sauce for the goose is sauce for the gander, as they say. I hope you'll come to understand that, before this day is done."

I hope I'll begin to understand before I get off this train, Jack thought.

"Charles, I need to borrow your phone," Jack said.

"And, if I don't want to give it to you?" Roast asked.

"I can find another. I could ask your father-in-law."

Roast pulled back his jacket and removed the cell

phone from his belt. Jack watched him carefully. He took the proffered device.

"I'll be right back," he said. "Talk amongst yourselves."

With that he walked down the aisle and descended to the lower level, leaving the two other men with dumbfounded expressions on their faces.

A few moments later, Jack was back. He handed the cell phone to Roast.

"Thanks," the private detective said. "Mind coming with me, to the scene of the crime? It will probably be easier to discuss the things that are on my mind with the evidence handy."

"And what if we don't want to come?" Roast asked.

"Aw, come on, Charles," the judge said. "Let's play the man's little game and follow along. Look at it as a sort of real-life version of that mystery game. You know the one, with the rope and the candlestick and all, in a big mansion. All the suspects are named after a color. Very entertaining."

"I haven't a clue," Roast said, and looked confused when Jack and the judge burst out laughing.

Jack stood back and allowed both men to precede him out of the dome. The judge went first. The going was slow.

Outside, night was beginning to fall. The train slowed and then stopped. They were sitting on a short siding. The brief lull made negotiating the stairs a little easier on the older man.

Jack had other reasons to be glad.

Chapter Twenty

Jack stopped just outside the little room where Oscar Dempster had died. He called to the two men ahead of him to stand with him.

Heads turned and watched as Jack began to speak. Then they turned away.

"Now, gentlemen, this is not a court of law. Anything I say is purely conjecture. It's an opinion, much like your opinion about a certain miscarriage of justice, Judge Marshall.

"For the sake of argument, let's just assume that it has been shown that you had a motive for murder. Let's assume that you had the means to bring it all about."

"How about we don't assume anything, and you just tell us what you think happened," Marshall said.

194

It was apparent that the elderly jurist was getting amazing pleasure from making Jack prove his case. But he was not arguing against anything Jack was saying. He didn't appear to be defending himself from complicity.

The private detective continued.

"Let's look at the matter of opportunity, first. I don't imagine it would have mattered much if Oscar hadn't come to the washroom to wash up, maybe shave, and comb his hair. You could have caught up with him in the vestibule or lured him away from Ruby somehow, Judge.

"You were fortunate—if that is really the spin we want to put on it—that Dempster decided to pull out his shaving kit and head back here. It told you exactly what he intended and where he would be. He opened the door when he was through, and you caught him off guard."

"Since we're theorizing here, Jack, let me throw this into the mix," Marshall said. "How about he came back here and left the door unlocked while he washed up."

"Are you telling me that that is what happened?"

"You figure it out. I'm done. I do appreciate, though, that you think I have the strength to overpower a man bigger, and somewhat younger, than I."

The thought hadn't occurred to Jack that to subdue Oscar Dempster, without arousing the suspicion of others, his assailant would have to be stronger, or very lucky.

"Alright then," he said. "You came up behind him and immobilized him. You covered his mouth with a towel or a handkerchief. You couldn't take the chance that he might cry out in alarm or in pain. And you gave him a shot with a stun gun."

"Now, Jack. Work with me on this, son. Where do I get this stun gun you're talking about? I want to see you work that one out."

"It wouldn't be hard to bring one onto the train," Jack said. "None of us had to go through a scanner before we got on the train. When you think about it, it's relatively easy to get weapons on board, as long as they're concealed.

"You could have brought a knife, but that's messy. A gun would shed blood too. And it would have made enough noise to arouse attention. You might have bought your own little zapper, but I suspect you decided to use the resources at hand."

"Mind if I sit down? I'm getting tired from standing," Marshall said.

"Sure. Let's all sit right here."

Jack indicated two seats that had been turned to face each other, and the trio sat down. Jack continued, a little unsure of where he was headed with what was, now, simply theory based on the things he had observed.

"What resources were at hand?" the judge asked.

"I suspect the two of you engineered that last night."

"How so?" Roast asked, rather unconvincingly, Jack thought.

"You've been covering up ever since you got on this train. You've avoided investigating any suggestion of foul play because you knew, even before you got on, that there had been foul play.

"You've lied about who you are and why you are here," Jack said. "I was wondering why you kept back some important details about who you really are. And now that I have some answers—unexpected ones, as it turns out—I'm convinced that you know exactly what happened in that coach, back there, this morning.

"This is the way I suspect that things went down. I think that you, Judge Marshall, came to the realization that Oscar Dempster was on the train. I don't know whether you were tracking his whereabouts beforehand, or whether you came to the realization when he got on the train with Ruby, yesterday. In either case, you would have had to work out a plan rather quickly, depending on where on the train Oscar and Ruby had been placed.

"However it happened, you called Charles from the train and asked him to meet you when we stopped for the evening. You had him come to your hotel room.

"Because you, Charles, weren't trying very hard to avoid being seen, either when you were arriving or leaving, last night, Ruby caught sight of you. Something about you attracted her attention. At the same time, you were able to see Oscar. Earlier today you made a comment that made me suspicious. You said, 'Oscar Dempster looked healthy enough to me,' or words to that effect. I wondered when you might have seen him alive.

"In any case, when you came into the coach this morning, Ruby Dempster recognized you. She told me, when I was speaking to her after Oscar's death, that she wanted to ask you a question. But, you have made yourself scarce most of the day, and she was feeling, I suspect, that perhaps it was a foolish question. So, she didn't get the opportunity to catch you in your little game.

"Of course, Oscar had kept his wife in the dark about his conviction for manslaughter all these years. He had moved to California after he got out of prison, and started a whole new life."

"So how do you suppose I was instrumental in all this? You really have no proof. It's all just conjecture," Roast said.

"While the two of you were together last night," Jack continued, "Charles passed his police-issue ECD to you, Judge Marshall. You used it to immobilize Oscar before strangling him to death. Then you passed it back to your son-in-law, probably during an opportune moment this afternoon."

"What makes you draw a conclusion like that?" Charles Roast asked.

"When I came up for one of my many opportunities for male bonding, you were speaking on your phone. You put it back in its holster, and I noticed there was no stun gun on your belt. When I borrowed your cell phone a little while ago, I noticed that you had your ECD and its clip-on case back where it belonged. I just had to ask myself, where was it before, and how did it get back into its holder?"

The officer made no attempt at an explanation.

The train had begun to move again.

With night drawing closer, it was becoming difficult to see what was outside the windows. The day, and the trip, would be over soon enough.

Jack wanted to finish dealing with the sad case of Oscar Dempster as well, but he still had evidence to present in the case that Judge Marshall was pressing him to prosecute.

"I don't suppose you gave any consideration to the possibility that someone might decide to investigate the man's death before Charles arrived."

Jack indicated Nadia Vukasovich, sitting a few seats ahead of them.

"When that young woman, who is a medical student, joined me in an examination of the body, we discovered the marks left by the probes from the stun gun. Then we saw the clumsy attempt to make it all look like a suicide. There was a broken clothes hook, so the man could not have hung long enough to strangle before it pulled away from the wall, if he'd done it himself."

"So you have some sort of theory," Roast said.

Judge Marshall was sitting with a slight smile on his wrinkled face.

"I think that, once Oscar was immobilized, it was a simple matter to slip a noose over his head. Where Judge Marshall made his error was in the assumption that he could pull Oscar up from the floor by himself. As he's already said, he doesn't have that kind of strength against Dempster's bulk. And then he overestimated the strength of the anchors holding the hook to the wall.

"Whether he strangled Oscar Dempster before trying to haul him off the floor or after the hook broke, it only involved keeping the tension on the end of the rope and closing off his wind pipe until he asphyxiated. It would be a simple matter to stand over him and to hang on until he stopped breathing.

"Then, Judge, you slipped out of the room and returned to your seat. With folks walking back and forth, getting ready for the day's trip, you would hardly have been noticed.

"Of course, if someone had been waiting, it would have been you, Judge, rather than Mr. Benson who would have run down the aisle, screaming."

"That's a fascinating story, I'm sure, Jack. But that's all it is, just a story," the officer said.

"Oh, shut up, for heaven's sake, Charles. The man has almost figured things out. Quit trying to defend me. You're a lousy lawyer," the judge said, a look of disgust on his face. "Go on, Jack. What else have you got to bolster your case? I must confess I'm impressed by your ability. Good show."

Jack motioned to Stewart to join them at the end of the coach.

When the young man had joined them, Jack said, "The three of us have been discussing Mr. Dempster's unfortunate death. When you and I were speaking earlier you mentioned that Judge Marshall had been a great help to you. I'd like you to repeat what you told me."

Stewart looked from face to face with a quizzical look before beginning. "Well, if it hadn't been for the judge, we might not have had Officer Roast here quite so quickly. Before I had a chance to do anything, he was right there, and offered to call the authorities. Said he had some pull with the powers-that-be, to use his term. He said he realized we were working on a tight schedule, and he could get someone on board who would accompany us so we wouldn't have to stop the train."

"Interesting," Jack said. "And can I assume you hadn't been to the back of the coach yet?"

"Why, no, err, yes. You can assume that. The alarm had only just been raised by Mr. Benson." He pointed to where the man was seated. "And then Mrs. Dempster started to yell. Things were getting pretty hairy in a hurry. I was glad of any help I could get."

"So, what did you do?"

"I thanked the judge, and accepted his offer."

Judge Marshall nodded affirmation.

Stewart continued, "Then I called the head end to let the engineer know we were to stop at the next available place with access to a highway. They told me where that would be, and I relayed the information to Judge Marshall. The rest, as they say, is history."

Jack thanked Stewart and sent him on his way. The coach attendant looked confused by the interrogation.

"Tell me, Judge. Why are you doing this?" Jack asked, once Stewart was out of ear shot. "Why are you confessing to murder? Don't you realize the consequences?"

Marshall crooked a finger at Jack, indicating he should draw closer. When the ear of the private eye was close enough to hear his whisper, the judge said, "Maybe I'm covering up for someone else."

He pushed Jack away by the shoulder and laughed the laugh that had become his signature.

"I'm serious, William. I don't get it."

"All in good time, son. All in good time," the judge said. "You have the necessary information to answer your own question. Of course, the answer may not seem as logical to you as it does to me. And, believe me, I've put a lot of thought into this. But enough about me, for now. What else have you got to throw into the mix? I like a good prosecution argument."

"As we've just heard, shortly after the discovery of Oscar's body, you went to Stewart and told him you could save the company a whole lot of inconvenience if he would let you call the police. You said you had pull with the authorities, and it wouldn't be necessary to stop the train while the investigation was going on."

Marshall tented his fingers in front of his mouth and nodded.

"You called Charles. You asked Stewart where would be the next spot with road access, and probably suggested that it not be a major town along the route. You gave that information to your son-in-law so he could meet the train.

"Charles. You had your wife drive you to the clearing where we stopped. When you spoke to the trainman, you probably told him that you had everything under control and that it would be best to let you communicate with the authorities and handle any questions. That would ensure that there was less of a chance that a real investigation would be launched before we arrived at Calgary.

"In your mind, you were in the process of protecting the innocent and administering justice. The innocent one was Billy Marshall. And, by the time you arrived, Oscar Dempster had met his end. Justice, to your perverted way of thinking, had been served."

"Your mistake—and, I'll admit, I didn't catch on to it until a while ago—was to reveal that you knew the name of the victim. You wouldn't have asked for that sort of information before leaving the police station. Dispatch, if they had been involved, would only have told you that there was a man down on the train and that you were to investigate.

"Stewart remembers that he was very careful not to give you too much information. He had the mistaken impression that you would want to make your own discoveries. But you blundered down the aisle, talking about the Dempsters by name."

"Suppose I said I was told the man's name by Judge Marshall," said Roast.

"Well, of course, you were," Jack said. "He called your cell, bypassing anyone else in the department who might later question the whole operation. But you knew his name long before he called, long before this whole plan was ever thought of.

"Those cell phones of yours were also a clue. Not at first, though. I thought the judge was canceling speaking engagements when the train was delayed. Then the calls became too frequent for that to be the case.

"I gave you, Charles, too much credit and thought that you were carrying out police business.

"The Guthries, over there, caught wind of your messaging by pure chance. That ringtone, Judge, caught the attention of a couple of believers in extraterrestrials. The volume of your phone made them think they were hearing aliens. Their unfounded suspicion led me to my conclusion. You were working on a coverup."

"That's only partly true," Marshall said, but gave no further explanation.

"Have I got it right?" Jack asked.

"Time will tell, son. Time will tell," the judge said.

"I was hoping that you would tell," Jack said. "I'm still trying to figure out why you are being so open about all this."

As it would turn out, the private investigator would not have long to wait.

Chapter Twenty-one

Suddenly the door at the far end of the coach was pulled open violently.

A mountain of a man, in a dark suit, stood within inside the coach, surveying the shocked faces of the passengers.

"I'm Sergeant Kiefer Unwin, Calgary Police. Which one of you is Elton?"

Jack raised his hand, as if this were the first day of class. Unwin homed in on him and started down the aisle. He patted his pockets as he came, looking for something. He stopped in front of the little trio, pulled open his suit jacket, and inserted a finger into an inside pocket.

"Ah, there it is. I'm always losing that thing. Liked it better when we pinned them on," he said, as he drew a leather folder from his jacket and flipped it open so Jack could see the badge and the I.D. card.

"I'm Elton," Jack said. "I'm sorry. I left my badge in my other jacket."

"What's this I hear about a murder?" the man asked.

Some of the other passengers were not as well informed as Unwin. They had not heard about a murder. They looked shocked.

An undernourished young man in a better-fitting suit had come down the aisle while the other officer was asking his question. He was introduced as Officer Claude Inglis.

Jack explained the situation to both men, while Marshall and Roast looked on.

"You told the dispatcher that you thought you had found the culprit," Unwin said, looking around the coach. He lowered his voice, and asked, "Who is it?"

"It's him," Jack said, pointing to the judge.

Marshall raised his hand and waved feebly at the two officers.

"This is Judge William Marshall," Jack said. "The other gentleman is Officer—and I use that term with serious reservation—Charles Roast, from B.C."

"I remember you," Inglis said, pointing at Marshall. "You're the 'Hanging Judge'."

You've got that right, Jack thought.

As if to confirm the private eye's assessment, Marshall replied, "I confess."

Whether he was agreeing to the moniker or agreeing

with Jack's conclusion was unclear. It apparently escaped Unwin that he should ask.

"Let me get this straight, Elton," Unwin said. "Someone has died on this train. You suspect foul play. And, you are prepared to accuse a former judge of the federal court of committing the crime if, in fact, a crime has been committed."

"That's about the size of it," Jack said. "And I suspect that the other man is an accomplice."

"Well, now. That's a pretty big accusation to make. We'd better be sure of our facts before we proceed, don't you think?" Unwin asked.

Jack nodded agreement.

"Judge Marshall. You too, Mr. Roast," Unwin said. "I don't want you to say another word. I need to advise you of your rights. I know you know what they are."

"And I'll listen quietly while you rehearse them for us," Marshall said. "I'll let you know if you get 'em wrong."

The jurist sat back, and listened attentively, eyes closed, while the sergeant rhymed off the rights of those about to be questioned. He concluded with, "Do you understand these rights?"

Both men nodded and kept silent.

"We should probably see the alleged victim before we go any further," Unwin said. "Inglis, I'm going to leave you here with His Honor and Mr. Roast. Elton, you come with me."

"Can I bring a medical expert?" Jack asked.

"Sure. The more the merrier. Lead on," Unwin replied.

As they went toward the door, Jack tapped Nadia on the shoulder and motioned that she should follow. She turned from the window, unfolded her legs from under herself, and took up the rear of the little procession.

When they arrived in the next coach, Unwin turned toward Jack.

Nodding at Nadia, he asked, "Can we talk freely?"

"Yes. I'm sure we can. This young lady knows the value of confidentiality. She will need to be able to exercise it in her medical practice."

"First of all, Jack, thanks for calling us on this one."

Unwin stuck out a meaty right hand. Jack grasped it and shook it.

"It's good to see you again," the police officer said. "I thought you'd given up on the police business. I heard there had been some rough spots in your career."

"Good to see you too. I think the problems sort of got ironed out. Officially, I drive a desk most days. But I still help out, from time to time. I never expected to be involved with this one, though. I'm supposed to be on my honeymoon."

"Hey, congratulations, guy. I hope I'll get to meet the 'little woman' before we get off this wagon train."

"Don't let Val hear you using that 'little woman' language. I married a cop, Kiefer."

"Oops. Sorry. Well, then, let's get to the subject at hand. What do we know?"

As they walked to the room where Oscar Dempster's body was stored, Jack filled Officer Unwin in.

"Caucasian male. Mid to late seventies. Well-fleshed. Smoker. Drinker. With heart complications. Died of asphyxiation as a result of ligature obstruction of the wind pipe. Have I got it right, doctor?"

Jack looked at Nadia.

"Sounds close enough, to me," she said, with a grin. "The guy was strangled with a rope, to put it in medical terms. But first he was immobilized by an electroshock device."

"Electrifying," Unwin said, picking up on the dark humor. "Let's have a look."

Jack found the trainman, who unlocked the door to the small room and retreated hastily to the little office where he had been filling out reports.

Together, the two men unwrapped the package that contained Oscar Dempster. The air conditioning had almost done its job of slowing the process of decomposition.

All agreed that it was fortunate that the city, with its morgue and its sealed coolers, was almost in sight.

"See here," Jack said, turning the body on its side. "Those marks are from a device like a Taser ECD. The intention was to render him unconscious and avoid a struggle, I figure."

"Whether that's all it did, can't be determined without an autopsy," Nadia said.

"What do you mean?" Unwin asked.

"The perpetrator obviously didn't read the safety warnings for using an ECD. Mr. Dempster had a heart problem. He was on medication for it. Anyone within range of his voice heard him talk about that yesterday.

"A shock like that, unexpected as it was, would have a double effect. First, there would be the surprise of being caught unaware. The heart races. There are other physiological changes. Some people scare very easily. It takes its physical toll.

"Then there is the electrical pulse itself. For a healthy person, it causes a certain amount of temporary paralysis and spasms. It can set up a far worse reaction in the less healthy body. If the ECD is abused, whether intentionally or not, it can have unintended results.

"I don't think it killed him, but I think it had a more powerful effect than just incapacitating him. It likely made him easier to kill."

"Is that important?" Unwin asked.

"It is, when you consider your suspect back there," Jack said.

He indicated the coach where Judge Marshall and Charles Roast were keeping Inglis company.

"He's not the strongest guy in the world, so if he managed to choke Oscar with a noose, he had some assistance from nature. Dempster didn't recuperate soon enough to fight him off."

The big policeman nodded.

"All the signs that I see indicate strangling," Nadia said, indicating the bulging eyes and protruding tongue.

"It was a slow death, as opposed to the quick end provided by what they call the long drop when administering a judicial hanging.

"In that case, the long fall snaps the neck. The theory is that it is quick and painless. No one who's been hanged has ever brought evidence to the contrary."

"It wasn't quick, and it wasn't suicide," Jack said. "His hands were free, and the will to live, plus the experience of slowly strangling, would have driven him to rethink his method, if he had been intent on ending his own life. He was sitting on the floor when we found him. He would have had no tension on the rope to make loosening it difficult, if he had been in control of the situation."

"But, you'll admit that there could possibly be circumstances where someone could have changed their mind but had other things prevent them from getting out of the situation?" Unwin asked.

"Sure," Jack said. "But there's one other thing."

"What's that?" the officer asked.

"Marshall says he did it."

"That is certainly something I intend to pursue with His Honor, once we've finished here. Let's make it quick," the officer said.

Kiefer Unwin completed his examination of Oscar Dempster, making notes in a small spiral notebook that he replaced in his shirt pocket when he was finished.

He and Jack rewrapped the body and turned out the

light. Jack called on the trainman again. He came and locked the door.

The little procession made its way back to the tourist-class coach where the other three men were waiting, along with the rest of the passengers from that car.

The street lights of the city moved past the windows. The train was pulling into the station. Soon it would be stopping for the night.

Until there was a resolution to the question of who was responsible, Jack knew the passengers could not leave. There was potential for a major confrontation. He was glad of the imposing presence that was Officer Kiefer Unwin.

The law man moved his bulk over toward a window and looked out.

Straightening up, he asked for attention, before announcing, "Ladies and gentlemen. We find ourselves in the midst of a police investigation. Your assistance and cooperation will be valuable to the process. I must ask you to remain in your seats until we have had the opportunity to speak to each of you and have determined that you can leave."

A collective gasp ran up and down the coach. A few angry voices could be heard already.

He continued, "We hope to make this process as quick as possible. I don't expect that it should take much longer than. . . . What shall we say, Officer Inglis, an hour or two?"

Sounds of mutiny were becoming evident. Violence

was being threatened. It appeared a bad situation was getting worse.

Jack looked down the coach to where Val was sitting. She looked back at him, and shook her head. She did not appear too happy with her lot.

And then Judge Marshall turned to Officer Unwin.

"Let 'em go. I have all the information you need. They don't need to stay. We can get this over with now."

Chapter Twenty-two

"What do you mean let them go?" Unwin asked. We need to get statements. We need to look for witnesses. Maybe someone has pertinent evidence.

"Surely, you're not really saying you are a murderer, Your Honor? You know, as well as I, that you are innocent until proven guilty."

"Are you arguing with me, Officer? I have spent more years in administering the law than you have breathing. You've advised me of my rights. I fully understand them. I choose to give up my right to remain silent. I'm prepared to act on my own behalf, which may label me a fool, but doesn't make me stupid. Yes. I fully intend to accept responsibility for Oscar Dempster's death."

"I will, at least, need to get contact information for

all these people before I dismiss them. We may need to talk to them again," Unwin said.

"Do what you must, but don't force them to stay, when there is no real reason for it. Trust me. You won't need their statements. I do not intend to launch any kind of defense."

Officer Inglis was given the task of collecting information. He was aided in his task by Stewart, the coach attendant, who provided a passenger manifest and introduced the constable to each of the people on the list.

After she had been interviewed, Nadia Vukasovich approached Jack and said, in a hushed voice, "Would it be all right if I stayed to hear what happens? I feel as if I have a personal stake in the outcome."

The private eye nodded to her and indicated a seat out of the flow of traffic.

One by one passengers filed down the aisle of the coach.

Some made a point of looking at the little man who had as much as admitted that he had taken the life of one of their fellow passengers. Some expressions were sad. Some looked angry.

There were still others who hurried off without giving a single glance to William Marshall.

Jack had not noticed, until now, that the train had come to a full stop.

Outside the window, the concrete platform stretched

the length of the row of cars. Light standards illuminated the way to the exits into the terminal.

At the foot of the stairs from the coach, Stewart stood, smiling a strained smile, as passengers stopped to thank him for his help and service over the past two days. It was clear from his expression that he was not convinced that the trip had been a total success.

Valerie came down the aisle with Ruby Dempster and helped her down the stairs.

Officer Inglis was close behind and assisted the woman along the platform.

Unwin looked at Jack, who was showing some serious concern for the woman's welfare.

"It's okay," he said. "She doesn't need to be here for this. Claude will take her to a waiting room where she can freshen up and have a cup of tea. A female officer will tend to her needs until we can get to her with any questions we might still need to ask."

Val had returned to the coach and took a seat across the aisle from the medical student. She reached across the space between them and, with a smile, quietly introduced herself before focusing her attention on the scene a few seats ahead.

When the last of the departing passengers had gathered their hand luggage and bid the *Last Spike Special* a final farewell, Stewart remounted the steps and closed the Dutch doors in the vestibule, top and bottom. He entered the coach and took a seat toward the back of the little group awaiting the unfolding of whatever was to come next.

Finally, Kiefer Unwin turned and addressed them all.

"Those of you who are staying for this are only being allowed to remain because you have had intimate contact with today's events. I do not have to let you stay if you say or do anything to inhibit my work or that of my colleague, who will rejoin us shortly.

"I will be addressing the two gentlemen who are with me here at the front. They have rights that must be respected and can ask to have any of you removed without giving a reason, as long as your presence is not instrumental to what will be happening here. Please do not make this harder than it already is."

Turning to Judge Marshall and Charles Roast, he said, "Your Honor, you don't have to do this here. You don't have to have any witnesses. We can go elsewhere or send them all away, if you prefer."

The judge looked around the coach and smiled.

"No," he said. "I think this will be fine.

"Jack, here, has been instrumental in investigating the alleged crime. This young lady"—he pointed toward Nadia—"is a medical expert of sorts who may prove valuable regarding some evidence you don't yet have at your disposal. She should stay."

Nadia looked from Jack to Val and back again. She shrugged and sat back in her seat.

The judge continued, "Stewart, back there, is an employee of the railway and probably should stay. And I believe this lovely young woman is a police officer, as well as Mr. Elton's wife. I don't think they should be separated any more than necessary."

"Alright," Unwin said, "let's get on with this."

"Very well," Marshall said. "To begin with, Jack Elton has, quite correctly, inferred that Oscar Dempster died at the hands of another. I am willing to admit now, that I am that person."

"But why?" Unwin asked. "Why did you do it? And why are you confessing so readily?"

"That was my question," Jack said.

"You'll find me to be a strange animal, much as those who have grown to know me have discovered, Officer."

"I believe in the law, and I have worked to bring justice for many years. It was my job to work within it and to do the best I could to be sure everyone was treated with fairness.

"Having said that, I confess to the human frailty of wanting revenge for those things that touch me personally. It has been relatively easy to pass sentence according to the law, when the victim and the accused were not part of my personal circle of acquaintances. That is as it should be. That is why I would recuse myself from any case that I might have a personal stake in. That is why I could not sit in judgment of a case that involved the death of my own son. The law doesn't allow for that. Conflict of interest, you know.

"When Oscar Dempster ran down my Billy with a

stolen car, I wanted to kill him with my bare hands for what he did to my family. When the system didn't mete out appropriate justice, I was madder still.

"That hatred never went away. I was determined to hunt him down and administer the punishment I thought he deserved right from the beginning."

"So why now?" Jack asked. "What changed so that you didn't feel any hesitancy to put yourself on the wrong side of the law you had vowed to uphold?

"I'm sorry, Kiefer. I didn't mean to take over your job," Jack added.

"That's all right. Would you answer that question, please, Your Honor," the big man said.

"Well, for one thing, I was too busy before now. To be frank, I didn't have time to spend in jail."

"But you've put yourself in a position where you can't escape that fate anymore," Unwin said. "Assuming you are found guilty, you will be given the prison sentence that was such a deterrent to you, until now. On top of that, you have done nothing to try to avoid that fate by all you've confessed this evening."

"Before I say anything else, I want to say to you, Charles, that I am deeply sorry for having drawn you and Heather into this affair. I hope you can both forgive me for what I've done."

Roast hung his head. "I have chosen not to say anything else right now, Judge Marshall," he said. "I hope you will understand. And I'm sorry too. I understand what you are saying. But, like the officer, I'm wondering why you are pouring out all of this and locking yourself away by your own testimony."

"I believe that if you take a life, you should lose your life," Marshall said. "And I still believe in the literal sense of that statement.

"I won't spend time in prison. I don't expect I'm going to get to trial. But I do expect that I will receive my just punishment."

The judge reached into the pocket of a jacket he had put on before the train stopped.

"Grab him!" Unwin yelled. "Inglis. Check him for a weapon!"

Claude Inglis lunged at William Marshall, as if the old judge was a combatant in a television wrestling exhibition.

Marshall began to giggle and then to laugh. Tears ran down his wrinkled cheeks.

"Stop. Stop. For heaven's sake let me alone. I'm not going to kill myself. I'm just trying to get this."

He held up a small piece of paper.

Jack recognized it as a page from a doctor's prescription pad.

"What's that?" Unwin asked, once Officer Inglis had released his deathhold on Judge Marshall.

"It's my death sentence," the judge replied.

Chapter Twenty-three

For a moment, everyone sat in stunned silence.

"What are you talking about?" Charles Roast asked, finally.

Kiefer Unwin reached for the paper.

The judge snatched it away.

"Not yet," Marshall said. "All in due time."

"C'mon, pops. What is all this about your death sentence?" Roast asked his father-in-law.

"Yes. Please explain yourself," Unwin said.

"This," Marshall said, waving the slip of paper, "is what made up my mind to deal, once and for all, with Oscar Dempster. The man had already destroyed my life. The memory of what he has done, to me and my family, has been a constant companion since the day Billy died, smashed against that tree by that evil man in a stolen car.

"He should have been hanged by the neck until he was dead for what he did. But I couldn't bring myself to do it until this."

"And what exactly is that?" Unwin asked.

The old jurist held up the paper again and continued.

"I had been feeling my age, somewhat, so I went to see Dr. Busby for a checkup. He took some blood and checked me over. Said everything looked fine, but I should wait for the results of the hematology. So I went back to my daily routine.

"One morning, his secretary called and said the doctor would like to see me in his office. I knew that he wasn't calling me in so he could slap me on the back and say, Congratulations, Your Honor, you're as fit as a fiddle."

"What did he say?" Jack asked, and mouthed "sorry" to Unwin, who had been conducting the interrogation.

"You know, Jack," Marshall said, "I can't remember a lot of the preliminary stuff he said. But one word stuck in my mind and has stayed there ever since."

"And that was?" Unwin took back his position as chief interrogator.

"The word was *leukemia*," the judge replied.

Everyone was focused on the little man now. Those faces that were not sad-looking, were filled with questioning.

Marshall continued.

"After Dr. Busby had said that, I pretty much lost the train of the conversation. He said that nothing could be done about the condition, other than watch and wait."

The judge's eyes grew wide, and his face reddened.

"Can you imagine, in this day and age, a doctor telling you that you have a fatal disease, and then saying all that the medical profession is prepared to do is to watch you die?"

"I hardly think that is possible," Nadia said from the back of the small group.

Marshall appeared to ignore the comment.

"Once I heard that, and I knew that I had been given a death warrant, it was easy to decide that Oscar should pay the ultimate price for his crime. I'll admit that, from that point on, I had no hesitation in making my plans to kill him.

"Here I was, awaiting the passage of a death sentence that I did not deserve. My life was going to come to an end prematurely. I just figured that there should be some purpose in it, even if that purpose was only understood by me.

"I would be guilty of the murder of another human being. Under ordinary circumstances, that would mean time in prison. As I've already said, I do not relish a life behind bars. It was the deterrent that kept me from carrying out my murderous fantasies all these years. But, now I was going to suffer the death penalty. There appeared no chance of a reprieve. The doctor had said he was planning no action to prevent my ultimate demise.

"So, here I am. I am guilty. I will hire myself a good lawyer to keep me out of jail until my trial. I will put my affairs in order. I will prepare for my day in court, if I live that long.

"If I do go to prison, I figure it won't be for long. It will be a sort of 'death row' imprisonment, and then my life will be taken. I will have paid my debt to mankind. It is all quite neat, don't you agree?"

"Pops, you never told me. You never told Heather. If I had only known . . ." Roast said, in obvious emotional distress.

"I'm truly sorry that I got you involved in this, Charles. But I appreciate everything you have tried to do for me," Marshall said.

"I'm truly sorry to hear your sad news," Jack said. "I must say, though, that I believe you are misled in your thinking.

"Oscar Dempster was tried, convicted, and sentenced many years ago. In that system of justice you claim to revere, he served the sentence that was passed. He had paid his dues to society, whether we agree on the fairness of the sentence or not.

"If everyone took the law into their own hands, as you did, we would have chaos. It was to prevent just the sort of thing you are confessing to, that the court system was established and that persons like yourself were appointed as judges."

"Excuse me."

The voice came from the back of the little group again.

"May I ask Judge Marshall a question?" Nadia asked Kiefer Unwin.

"Well, I don't know," the officer answered. "Is it relevant to what we are doing here?"

"I was just wondering if the judge knows what the actual disease is that he suffers from."

"That's what this is for," Marshall said, waving his little prescription paper.

"Alright. Go ahead," Unwin said.

"The doctor said I had . . . let's see. I have a little trouble reading my own writing. He says I have something called chronic lymphocytic leukemia."

"I see," the medical student said. "And you say you had no previous symptoms?"

"That's right. A death sentence right out of the blue. And apparently there's no cure. Am I right?"

"And nothing has changed, as far as your health is concerned?"

"No. I'm feeling just fine," Marshall replied. "Doesn't much matter, though, I suppose. Leukemia is leukemia. I'll be dead soon.

"Well, Your Honor, I don't know whether I have good news or bad news or a little of both," the medical student said.

"What's that supposed to mean?" the judge asked.

"Yes, miss. If you have something to say that has a bearing on what we've heard, I'd like to know what it is," Unwin said.

"It's Nadia. And, yes, I think what I have to say is

important. At least it will be important for the judge to hear."

"Go ahead then. If I think it's irrelevant, I'll tell you to stop."

The young woman stood up and walked to the front of the coach. She looked directly at William Marshall.

"Sir, you should have paid closer attention to what was said when your doctor gave you your diagnosis. As I said, I don't know whether what I'm going to say will be good news or bad."

"What are you getting at?" Marshall asked.

"You, sir, are a classic zero stage chronic lymphocytic leukemia patient. We shorten the disease name to the letters CLL. I'll use that term to help keep this relatively concise.

"Cancer of the lymphocytes usually appears in people later in life. Most patients are men, and the disease strikes, usually, after age sixty-five. It is a disease of one of the white blood cells, as you have surmised. Interestingly enough, it is usually diagnosed in just the way you describe."

Unwin held up his hand.

"Excuse me, miss, um, Nadia. You're losing me here. I thought you said this was relevant. Could we move along, please?"

"Sorry. I'll do my best, but you need to hear some of this background information, I think."

Unwin nodded and waved his hand in a go-on gesture.

Nadia picked up her narrative. "Your illness, Judge

Marshall, is typically diagnosed by accident, when the patient goes for routine blood tests. That is when the elevated lymphocyte count is discovered. Like almost everyone who has been diagnosed as you were, the whole thing came to you out of the blue, so to speak. You had no symptoms.

"I said you should have paid better attention to your doctor. I need to tell you that you will, indeed, die. But, Your Honor, you are not likely to die for a good long while yet. I strongly suspect that, under the circumstances, that news may not bring you any great consolation."

"So, you're saying I'm going to die a slow, painful, death?" Marshall asked.

"Probably not," Nadia said.

Shock registered on the judge's face.

The countenances of the others in the group also exhibited surprise.

"I hate doctors. No offence intended, my dear," the old judge said. "When I get ill, I usually wait as long as possible before I have it checked out. I waited a long time before I went to have myself checked out. You know what they say about men and their health."

"No. What?" Nadia asked.

"Men won't go to see a doctor unless they have a fatal head wound," Marshall replied.

The soon-to-be doctor did not look impressed.

"If only you had been as bold to ask as you are to give advice, you might not be where you are now," she said. "You want respect for your own knowledge but have no respect for the wisdom of someone who wants to help you be healthy.

"I think what your doctor likely said was that there was no need to do anything about your disease. He wasn't giving up on you. He was giving you encouraging news or trying to," she added.

"If things remain as they are, it is not likely that you will die from this disease. It just requires that your doctor keep an eye out for the development of symptoms. So, the good news is the bad news too, I guess.

"Because you are not likely to die any time in the near future, you are likely to be able to serve out your full sentence, whatever that may be."

The young woman walked back to where she had been sitting, leaving everyone in stunned silence.

"Officer Inglis," Unwin said, "please let the others know that we are finished here. And loan me your cuffs, would you. Judge Marshall and Mr. Roast will be coming with us."

Inglis helped the sergeant affix the restraints to both men and then walked down the aisle, speaking into his radio in confidential tones.

"Thank you all for your patience," Unwin said to the small gathering. "I appreciate the work Mr. Elton has performed on our behalf today. And Miss Vukasovich, you are going to make a fine doctor, I am sure. Your little lecture has been enlightening, to say the least. I'm not sure that everyone here shares my enthusiasm."

Judge Marshall looked sullen. Now sitting with his hands cuffed in front of himself, he had lost all semblance of self-assurance.

Roast looked beaten. The realization that he had been an accessory to murder appeared to have settled on him heavily.

"You are all free to go," Unwin said. "We may need to get in touch with some of you at a later date. Please speak to Officer Inglis before you leave, if you haven't already done so."

He motioned Jack to wait. Val came up the aisle and sat beside him. She took his arm and rested her chin on his shoulder, hugging him tightly.

It's going to be alright, Jack thought.

"Thanks," he said.

"For what?" Val asked.

Jack smiled.

As she headed for the door, Nadia Vukasovich leaned over toward the newlyweds.

"I'll wait for you two in the station. I have a suggestion I hope you might consider," she said, and was gone.

"What was that about?" Val asked.

"I'm sure I don't know," Jack said. "I guess we'll see."

All the other passengers had left.

Stewart had returned to his little storage room to finish up his tasks for the evening. Supplies had to be replenished. The paperwork would wait while the coach attendant dealt with the platform workers anxious to get home after an evening of waiting for the late arrival of the *Last Spike Special.*

Outside the window, Jack saw two men in police uniforms pass by. Shortly he heard their heavy footfalls on the metal stairs of the coach. Officer Inglis had joined them in the vestibule and escorted them to where the two prisoners were sitting.

"You will go with these two officers now," Unwin said.

Marshall and Roast were helped to their feet and taken away.

Jack and Valerie watched through the window.

Unwin was suddenly beside them.

"So this is the new Mrs. Elton. Officer Elton, I gather. I'm so pleased to see that Jack is settling down," he said.

"I'm Val," she said smiling. "And I doubt that there is anything that will settle this man down. So far, he's spent most of our honeymoon trying to solve a crime."

"So I've heard," Unwin said.

"I'll change. Really I will," Jack said in a pitiful sounding voice. "At least, for the rest of our vacation," he added with a laugh.

"Would you take this man into custody, Officer Elton? And escort him off the train. Don't let him out of your sight. We don't want him to get away from you again."

"Yes, sir, Officer Unwin," Val said. "Trust me. I'll put him in cuffs if I have to. He's going to be sentenced to life—with me."

Val giggled and gave Jack a hug.

"And one more thing," Unwin said.

They both looked at the officer.

"I really do appreciate what you have done here—both of you.

"Jack, you overcame some pretty staggering opposition today. The judge says he intended to turn himself in, but you never know how that might have gone, if you hadn't pushed for answers. And then his son-in-law turned out to be a disgrace to the profession of officer of the law by helping with the commission of the crime. I think he's in for a severe sentence himself.

"And Val, it's rare to have someone as understanding as you were today. Thanks for giving Jack permission to do what he did. Between you and me, I think he's trainable. I wish you luck.

"Now, both of you, get out of my sight. Have a wonderful life together."

With that, he waved his hand in a dismissive gesture and hurried them off the train before returning to the coach.

As they walked down the platform, Jack looked back at the train.

"I guess he will be here for a while longer. There's the crime scene to deal with, and poor Oscar will need to go to the morgue. He'll have an appointment with the coroner tomorrow, I guess."

"Jack Elton," Val said sharply, "I don't want to think about police work for another ten days, at least. I'm on holiday. I consider it my sacred duty to make sure you are on holiday too. I'm still thinking about how you are going to make up the time I was without you most of today."

"How about South America?"

The voice came from behind them.

They turned together and saw a smiling Nadia, leaning against one of the light standards.

She came toward them and urged them both to walk toward the exit with her.

"What's this about South America?" Jack asked.

"Have you ever visited Argentina?" Nadia asked.

Jack and Valerie both shook their heads.

"It is a lovely country," she said. "You will find that it would be just the right place for a wonderful vacation. It is not like it once was. You can visit there without fear. I could tell you so much about my country, but it would be better for you to see it. I could be your tour guide."

"That sounds just wonderful," Valerie said. "But it would be expensive to take a trip like that, I would imagine."

"It would be worth it," the young woman said. "You could save up."

"Well, I did promise that I would make up for ignoring you," Jack said. "It's something to think about."

"You do that," Nadia said. "Here is my card. It has my address and phone number in Argentina. I have friends who have a lovely little hotel in Patagonia. I think they would be willing to give you a great deal, as a favor to me. Just get in touch when you are ready to visit. And remember one more thing."

"What's that," Jack asked.

"When it is winter here, it is summer in my country. You may want to consider that some December or January."

"I'm liking this more all the time," Valerie said. "Jack and I will have to have a talk about that."

"Now, you two have a honeymoon to attend to. No more work until you both get home. I will be going, for now. Write to me, and let me know when you will be visiting."

"We'll do that," Jack said, and held out his hand.

"There's something else you need to know about my country," Nadia said.

"What's that," he asked.

"When we say good-bye to friends, we don't do it like that."

With that she threw her arms around Jack and hugged him warmly. Then she went to Valerie, kissed her on the cheek and embraced her too.

"Hasta la vista, amigos," she said. "I look forward to seeing you again."

With that, she was gone.

Jack and Valerie were left standing alone on the platform.

"Well, I wonder what adventures await us in the big city," Jack said.

Valerie gave his arm a gentle punch.

"Mr. Elton, you are under arrest. Come quietly, or I may have to use force. You are sentenced to two weeks, give or take a day or two, of absolute rest with the occasional guided tour thrown in. You will eat exotic meals and fast food. You will stay up late and sleep in. You will laugh at inappropriate times, sing off-key, and avoid work at all cost. Now follow me, and don't argue."

"Yes, officer. Whatever you say, officer," Jack said, and gave Valerie a hug.

Then, the Eltons walked out of the train station and into the cool night air.

As they went, hand in hand, Jack's only thought was *It must be a crime to be this much in love.*